Lost

In The

Sins

Of Their

Mother

For Evelyn,
Thank you for
sharing my life
story. Dottie Bug

Lost In The Sins Of Their Mother

Co-Authors
Dottie Bug and Patti Cake

Written By
Keith Coachman

GMA Publishing

Copyright © 2003, Lost In the Sins of Their Mother Keith Coachman All rights reserved.

ISBN: 1-59268-054-2

GMA Publishing
Newburgh, Indiana

GMAPublishing.com
Check out our website
GMA is a global publishing company
Our books are available and distributed around the world and can be found on the internet at Amazon, Barnes and Noble and any major bookseller.

GMAPublishing@aol.com

All rights reserved. No portion of this book may be reproduced, stored in a retrieval system, or transmitted in any form or by any other means- electronic, mechanical, photocopy, recording or any other except for brief quotations in printed reviews, without the prior permission of the publisher.

Cover By: Cecilia Brendel
Manuscript Assistant: John Beanblossom
Cover Photographs By: James Bishop and Nancy Aldrich

Printed in the United States of America

Dedication

To Our Mother:

Through her life, she deceived us.

Through her death, she has set us free.

We love you, Mom.

Dottie Bug
And
Patti Cake

To the Reader

In February of 2001, a truly sad, but well overdue death was unfolding. The two had been married for almost 50 years, but neither the husband nor the wife had made any arrangements for a death. They had spent so much time focusing on how sick they were and trying so hard to out sick the other, that actually dying never crossed their minds. Her condition worsened by the hour. She floated in and out of coherence and unconsciousness. She blabbered incomprehensible one day, and she knew everyone in the room with her the next. The end of her life was approaching quickly. However, due to finances, the viable options were extremely limited. There were decisions that needed to be made and her aging and ailing husband was not much help. As he, too, was on his deathbed. Her daughters never left her side. On one of the good days, she was able to talk to her two daughters about the final arrangements and where she wanted to be buried. That is when Pandora's box opened wide. This whole saga started with three simple words.

"Next to Him".

50 years of suppressions, omissions, fallacies, and outright lies came flooding into their minds.

For fifty years, they had unknowingly led lives full of lies and deceit. The best way to describe how those three little words made them feel seemed to be summed up in just one word.

"Why?"

Why couldn't she tell them the truth? Why had their mother allowed this? Why did she carry her deep, dark secrets to her grave?

This is a true story about two little girls whose world came crashing in around them at ages five and two when their daddy was taken from them by death. For over 50 years, the *REAL* details of the events before then and since were never shared with either of them. Now, since their mothers death, and, since very few of the people involved are still living, others who have always known the truth are finally comfortable coming forward. Now, so long after the fact, the world can meet one of the most intriguing women that ever walked this earth.

Other than the names, there is nothing in the book that is intentionally false. This book contains facts that have been discovered since her death.

Many long hours traveling between cities and counties have verified all the information this book contains. Each bit of information has been verified through vital records, legal documents, eyewitness accounts, and sheer determination. The names have been changed to protect those still living that may not wish to be recognized. Nevertheless, they will know the truth when they read it, and nothing in this book can be disputed. Many years of questioning discrepancies in the stories that were told, and trying to put pieces of mind puzzles together drove the two girls to find the next answer. Each answer led to another question. Each question led to a new fact. Each new fact unfolded the story of a lady that both of them wished they could have known.

These two little girls grew up in less than ideal environments and such traumatic circumstances that 50 years would pass before they could face it. The two little girls are grown women with children and grandchildren of their own. Now, they can put closure to their past and move forward with the knowledge that they, too, are worthy of being loved.

Through this book, her daughters can rest assured that they upheld their mother's final request-

"Promise you won't let anyone forget me!"

Dottie Bug and Patti Cake

Preface from the Writer

My mom and aunt probably thought I was never going to complete this book. Every time I saw my mom the first thing from her lips was, "How's the book coming?" She said it with a smile, but I knew what she meant every time she said it. I explained to her that it took over 50 years to unfold this storyline and almost 2 years to gather enough information to answer the questions they had always been afraid to ask. They couldn't expect it to be written in less than a couple of months. I read the notes my mom and aunt had gathered and offered suggestions about the flow and order of the events. I offered to write the book as a story rather than a series of choppy notes obviously taken from two different- though similar- points of view. I was grateful to my mom and my aunt when they agreed to let me do this and soon I ended up getting so involved in the writing of the story that I felt like I was sitting in an IMAX theater all alone watching a movie about a woman I had never met.

I had been involved from the start but not from a research point of view. Rather, it was a spiritual point of view. I was close to my granny and she always considered me the son she never had.

Through out my life I had been privy to the many stories she loved to tell. Even though the stories often seemed farfetched, I loved to listen, just because I knew she loved to tell them. When reading the notes my mom and my aunt wrote, I realized that my granny was probably telling the truth. At least, I could see that the stories she told could have been possible. There was more to her than simply an old lady everyone in the county called *"Granny."*

She was a woman that was so common, yet so extraordinary. I could not help but wonder what the woman I knew as "Granny" had seen in her life. I wish I had been older so that I could have watched her life from an outsider's point of view. Every one that knew her felt the presence of a great lady. Everyone that knew her felt the strong and powerful spirit she possessed. Now that she is gone, all those that knew her smile when they think of her.

I visited my uncle in Ft. Lauderdale in June of 2003 to get away from my life in Atlanta, clear my mind and finally get the uninterrupted time I needed to complete this book. There, he and I talked in great lengths regarding the periods covered in the notes I read.

He grew up witnessing much of what happened and it was entertaining to hear a viewpoint that added even more credence to the notes my mom and aunt gave me. My uncle knew my mom, my aunt, and many of the events that molded the lives of these two little girls. He knew the neighborhood and told stories of his visits with my mom over the years. He was there the night my daddy got the phone call from Patti Cake, my mother, and his insight gave me a more vivid picture of these events, involving me even deeper.

I was determined to get this book finished this week. My mom jokingly said she would get a lawyer after me if she needed to. I had psyched myself up for it. I had all the pictures, notes, and the parts I had already started. I carried them on the plane with me just in case my luggage went to Alaska or something. The flight was loading. I was in row 10, seat A, so I knew I would be the last one on and I waited my turn to board the plane. When I got on Air Tran Flight 304 to West Palm Beach, a polite and big smiling attendant greeted me so I was already at ease. I made my way through the first class seats towards the curtain that separated "them" from "us" and when I looked up, I saw the face of the lady I had grown up knowing.

She looked so much like my grandmother that it was more scary than amazing. The thick, almost plastic in texture skin had the same lines of wisdom running around the most inquisitive, fun loving eyes. Her fine lips were painted the same orange frosted pink my grandmother used to wear. Her skin tone was pale, but anyone could see that she had been tan most of her life. The hair on her head was almost identical to my granny's. I smiled, remembering how my granny used to want her hair to look good whether it did or not. The once colored, now fading-back-to-gray semi curl outlined her face exactly like my granny's used to. But what really got me was the same hands and fingers that had shelled beans, pulled corn, canned tomatoes, pickled cucumbers and made some of the best jellies anyone had ever tasted. All the while, she spent hours every day, writing down in her journals every thought, every action, and every ounce of love she ever felt.

I couldn't help but to stare at her, hoping she wouldn't notice. I wanted to laugh, cry and keep staring. Instead, I directed my attention to the outside of the plane. As the plane took off, the view happened to be Shannon Mall, Highway 138, and the lake that she taught me how to fish in.

All those years of gardening, eating, endless summers, and God-only-knows how many memories. I took it all in as a sign that this book would be the legacy my mom, my aunt, and MY GRANNY deserve.

Keith Coachman

Contents

Chapter One	Amazing Grace	1
Chapter Two	A Humble Beginning	9
Chapter Three	The Soldier	14
Chapter Four	After the Annulment	18
Chapter Five	The Baby	23
Chapter Six	The First Few Years	31
Chapter Seven	Ending the Violence	39
Chapter Eight	The New Life	49
Chapter Nine	The Man At the Drive In	55
Chapter Ten	All in the Family	68
Chapter Eleven	A New Beginning, For One of Them Anyway	76
Chapter Twelve	Life Continues for Dottie Bug	82
Chapter Thirteen	Sisters Rejoin and Families Complete	87
Chapter Fourteen	The Sick Years	95
Chapter Fifteen	The Final Days	111
Chapter Sixteen	The Investigation	132
Chapter Seventeen	John Lewis Wyatt, Jr.	140
Prologue		154

Chapter One

Amazing Grace

"*AMAZING GRACE, HOW SWEET THE SOUND* that saved a wretch like me. I once was lost, but now I am found. Was blind but now I see."

The words to Gail's favorite song seem to have burned a hole in their consciousness, as if the words were seared into their very soul. Neither of them could stop humming this tune. Their Mother always loved it so much, so they requested it be played for her. After all, for once in her life, this day truly was all about her.

The historic little town of Fayetteville is located in middle Georgia and is considered by those that live there to be the heart of the Deep South. The town is always hustling with the traffic of the local residents who are still old fashioned enough to give their support to the locally owned businesses around the town square. In the very center of that busy little town square stands the majestic old two-story white stucco courthouse, which, to this day, is still the Fayette County seat, and host to some type of local fair, or exhibit, or art show for one of the local schools almost monthly.

Not much about Fayetteville, Georgia has changed in the past hundred and fifty years or so. It still looks as stately and impressive as ever. A few blocks east of the square is Jeff Davis Boulevard, an area where beautiful old Victorian homes still stand regal, as if time had never touched them.

Years ago, one of these old homes was converted to a well-known and prestigious funeral home. The large, freshly painted sign out front proudly reads "B.T. Howell & Sons Funeral Home". Upon entering, it is obvious why the locals hold this business- along with the well-mannered and professional staff, in such high regard. The walls are freshly painted, the floors immaculate, and the furniture looks as if it came right off the set of "Gone with the Wind".

There were folks moving back and forth, taking care of business like any other day of the week. It was February 26, 2001. The month was almost gone. The blue sky was crystal clear and the sun was shining so brightly you would think it was midday in spring, instead of late afternoon in winter. The front porch, or "the veranda" as old Southerners called it, was filled with people from all over the state. Brothers, sisters, aunts, uncles, nieces, nephews, children, grandchildren, and even great grandchildren took their turn with their quiet hellos and salutations. Even with the many friends that came to offer their support and condolences, it seemed more like a family reunion than a wake. Everyone spoke quietly with each other, occasionally letting out a chuckle. Everyone was reminiscing about their own favorite times- the big smiles that seemed to be permanently engraved on her face; the big hugs she gave you every time you saw her, regardless of how many times you saw her; and the love that emanated from her like a beacon in the night. Yes, it didn't matter whom she met, or how long she had known them, she was more than just "Gail". She was more than simply "Mama". To everyone she met, she was "Granny" and everyone loved Granny.

They had to. It couldn't be helped. It just happened. The littlest children ran around in the already emerging grass dispersing their nervous energy. Some of them were too young to grasp what was really happening. Even though their young hearts and minds knew and loved Granny, they could never realize how her passing would affect them. Gone was the giggling and laughing until the tears flowed. Time would pass and eventually they would forget the light that twinkled in her eyes every time you came to see her. They would never again taste Granny's canned green beans, the grape jelly she made from muscadines she had gone to *"the turse"* and picked or the home made pickles and chow-chow. Worse, yet, those poor little children would never know just how good a hot buttered biscuit really was.

Yes, the time had finally come. Granny Gail was gone. She left behind John Louis Wyatt, known to all the kids as "Papa". He had been her husband of forty-seven years, and a daughter named Jennifer Lynn Wyatt-Jameson. Oh, yeah, she also left behind two other daughters- Patricia Leighann Sanders-Coachman and Maria Diane Sanders-Monroe. Gail married Johnny when Dottie Bug was 5 years old and Patti Cake was eight. But, enough said about that right now. Between the three girls, they had given Gail 11 grandchildren and 14 great-grandchildren, all of whom she loved very deeply. Just after each girl was born, Gail had started calling Patricia "Patti Cake" and Diane, because she was so small when she was born, had always been called "Dottie Bug". This is the story of those two little girls- "Patti Cake" and "Dottie Bug".

"This is not the kind of day you want to attend a funeral," thought Patricia Leighann, the oldest daughter of Gail Leighann Martin-Sanders-Wyatt. The setting was just too pleasant to be a sad day. All the kids, grandkids, and great-grandkids, along with the extended family and a few friends made their way into the chapel of the prestigious old funeral home. It was time for the service to begin. Stan Martin, Jr., the oldest son of Gail's favorite

brother Stanley, was ordained as a Baptist minister many years ago and was the most obvious and appropriate choice to present the eulogy. Stan, Jr.'s words were strong and true, and even though some of his words offended the younger "yuppie" grandkids, Stan, Jr. spoke of the hard life Granny Gail and her family had always known. Her father and mother, Earnest Lloyd Martin and Annie Mae Martin, were never more than poor dirt farmers, raising eight children, and carving their living as tomato farmers on several acres of red Georgia Clay.

As they listened to the reflective nature of Stan, Jr.'s sermon, Dottie Bug could not help but wonder how much of their Mamas life did they *really* know? *"Mama has certainly left a legacy of mystery,"* Dottie Bug mused. Her thoughts and feelings ranged from sorrow that her mother was gone to true thankfulness that her pain and suffering was finally over. Dottie Bug wondered just how much of her mama's life her uncle Stanley had witnessed and wanted very desperately to talk to him later. She really wanted to pick his brain and get some funny stories about her mother when she was a young girl to put in the scrapbook she had begun so long ago.

Dottie Bug's thoughts were interrupted - the service was over and it was time to go. Once again, a musical rendition of

"Amazing Grace" began playing softly in the background as everyone stood. They all waited in the pews while the funeral directors closed the casket and gently wheeled Granny Gail out of the room and into the hearse at the lead of the funeral procession. The family quietly exited the funeral home and made their way to their respective vehicles. The shiny black car carrying the matriarch of the family slowly pulled out onto Jeff Davis Boulevard and proceeded north, towards Granny Gail's final resting place.

For many years, Jeff Davis Boulevard remained a small two-lane road. However, in the past few years, as Fayetteville grew in size, the road had expanded to a four-lane highway and the number of cars that traveled the road both frustrated and amazed the locals. However, the day of Granny Gail's funeral, the city and county police arrived in full force and a bystander probably got the impression that royalty had arrived. The patrol cars were cross parked on the streets, blocking both directions to make sure no one was going to intrude on this family's private state of grief.

It was so very touching to drive in such an amazingly long procession and watch as the traffic was completely stopped by officers standing at attention- their hats off and over their hearts. They may have never known this 77-year-old woman, but they, too, were showing their respect to "Granny Gail". Mile after mile, as the procession drove through town; each intersection was blocked off in much the same manner. Once outside the Fayetteville city limits, the Fayette County police picked up and continued opening the path. Even though the line of cars was over a mile long, the parade of mourners snaked though the county with nothing to stand in the way.

Dottie Bug was silent as she rode with her husband, not talking, only taking it all in. The only emotion she was cognoscente of was the absolute wonder at the truly touching sight of a little town she herself had never known and the dignity and pride this little town was showing to "her mama". They were treating her mama as if she was truly "somebody". You would have thought she was the Governor, himself.

The whole scene is still so vivid in Dottie Bug's and Patti Cake's minds, even today, so long after their mama has gone. Looking back on the outpouring of kindness and respect the town showed their mother the day she was carried to her final resting place, and given everything the two of them have since found out about their mama, one thought keeps going through their minds,

"How proud Mama would be to have all these attractive men so well dressed, standing at attention and bowing in her honor!"

Chapter Two

A Humble Beginning

ANNIE MAE WAS ABOUT TO deliver a baby just as she had three times before- at home and with nothing to alleviate the pain. In those days, there were no fancy hospitals in every neighborhood. There was only a county doctor who would come by periodically to check on the status of things, and hopefully, he would get there before the baby was born. That is, *IF he could get there*. Imagine the pain the women had to endure in those days!

It was New Years day, 1922 and times were very hard. Gail Leighann Martin came bouncing into this world shortly after midnight, making her birthday *technically* January 2, 1922. Its funny how things get screwed up. All her life, Gail celebrated her birthday on January 1st, New Years Day. Her family always celebrated her birthday the same way. That is, until she reached the age of sixty-two! She was signing up for Social Security and she needed a "certified" birth certificate. It was then that she found out from the State of Georgia birth records that her mother had lied to her so many years ago. The reason? She had wanted so badly to have a New Years baby, and since she only missed it by a couple of hours, she decided that she would *have* her a New Years Baby!

Gail's father was born Ernest Lloyd Martin. In his later years, everyone he met knew him as "Pappy Lloyd". He was the typical "dirt farmer", making his living by planting acres and acres of tomatoes that were later harvested and sold at the State Farmers Market. At one time, Mama Mae's family had very lucrative earnings growing, picking, and selling cotton.

However, Pappy Lloyds bad decisions and greed left him with barely the land he planted, and they now lived in an old four-room house that sat on big rocks in the middle of the very fields he worked so hard to maintain. The house had no insulation and the cracks in the floors were so big you could count the chickens under the house. There was no indoor plumbing, and the old wood-burning stove was the only heat they had in the long cold winters. They never had a telephone, and this was many years before television was around. Only an elite few in the county even had a radio. Pappy Lloyd and Mama Mae never had electricity or running water, yet, somehow, the Martin family managed to survive year after year.

The offspring of Lloyd and Annie Mae Martin eventually grew to eight children. This was a mixed blessing for the times, because even though food was scarce and work was hard to come by, such a large family did provide many hands to help in the fields. Gail was the fourth of the eight kids, and she, like the other kids, was required at an early age to work in her daddy's tomato fields along side the adults. Gail's job was to walk behind her mama, up and down the long rows of freshly planted tomatoes watering each one as it was placed in the ground. Acre after acre was walked as she watered little tomatoes from sun up to sun down. Her young legs had walked several miles before the day was gone.

Gail was never allowed to be "girlie", so she ended up being quite the "tomboy". When she wasn't working in the fields, young Gail loved to hang around with her favorite brother Stanley. He was younger than her and his friends, but she could climb trees better than most of the boys. She loved wrestling and could often be found out behind the barn hiding with the neighborhood boys and getting into trouble. In fact, by the time she was seven, she could smoke an entire pack of cigarettes without even choking! Yes, she enjoyed playing rough, and stories have been told of how many times she would "whoop the tar" out of the neighborhood bullies for picking on little Stan.

Pappy Lloyd needed all the help he could get picking tomatoes, so Gail had to quit school after the seventh grade. Her daddy knew she wouldn't have any trouble getting a man later, so he didn't think she needed the education. All the while not knowing just how right he was. By the time she was 13, she was already tall and lean. All the years of working outside had turned her long wavy hair to strawberry blond and her skin was bronzed from the sun she was constantly exposed to. Before anyone even noticed it was happening, she was blossoming into a woman. Her whole life began to change as the adolescent hormones began initiating shapes and curves in certain areas of her body. Things began to happen that would forever change the rest of her life.

Since her daddy had taken her out of school, the young woman she was becoming no longer had to think about the homework she had always toiled over by the light of the fire. Instead, more mature thoughts began creeping into her mind, and the crowded four-room house began to close in on her. Eventually, her mind was made up. The house she shared with her large family closed in on her for the last time, and she decided to hitch a ride into town and get away from it for a while.

A few hours passed and no one noticed their sister was missing. Suddenly, her oldest Brother, Calvin, known to everyone as "Brother" came running into the house shouting, *"Daddy! Daddy! You got to come get Gail! She's down at the honky-tonk dancing on the tables with nuthin but her panties and brassiere on! Hurry! Before she gets into more trouble!"*

Yep, Gail had found the FIRST true love of her life - *dancing*!

Chapter Three

The Soldier

GAIL WOULD SNEAK OUT OF the house and go dancing every chance she got. Benny Goodman had just been named "King of Swing" and Gail was the Queen as far as she was concerned. All her life, she used to say that she could always "cut the rug" better than anyone else! None of the other girls had her swing. She knew how to move her 13-year old hips and the boys went crazy! She learned early in life how to use the body of a woman, knowing when to tease, and when to please! She soon became the heartthrob of every boy in the county. It was amazing how even as young as she was, everyone fell so quickly infatuated with her!

With her newfound skill, staying at home just wasn't an option anymore! She worked hard finish her daily chores and played even harder when the work was done. As often as she could, she would talk one of her brothers into taking her to the honky-tonk to find some excitement. Pappy Lloyd had pretty much given up on her. He threatened several times to send her to the reformatory, but, try as he may, he just couldn't find a way to keep her away from the boys!

One weekend, her brother Calvin came home on a furlough from the Navy, bringing with him a friend of his from the service. When Calvin introduced an impressionable young Gail to Maxwell Jackson, her hormones went racing to places that only the heart can find. He was the most handsome man she had ever seen. He was taller than she was, and very muscular. His eyes were dark and sparkled with merriment behind deep tanned skin and dark, naturally curly hair. She wondered if he was Italian. She began to dream and her dreams were big!

In the weeks after he arrived, Gail fell deeply in love with Maxwell Jackson and she didn't care who knew it! She dreamed of spending the rest of her life with him. Somewhere. Somehow! So what if she was only 13? She felt like a woman. In fact, she looked like a woman. Gail made up her mind, and no one was going to stop her. Not even Pappy Lloyd. Gail had decided to sweep Max off his feet so fast he would never know what hit him.

Max had never met a woman like Gail before. He saw sparkles in her dreamy eyes, emanating the sexual fire in her soul. She was definitely sure of herself and Max was in love with everything about her. He loved her from the top of her strawberry blond hair to the tip of her long skinny toes. He loved the sprinkling of freckles that dotted the top of her nose, the only sign of the innocence of her age. Every time he looked into her eyes, his heart was set on fire. He was absolutely clueless that she was only 13. She had a pure, raw, sex appeal that drove him crazy mad! He had to have her! He quickly whisked her away to the next county and took her for his bride; just knowing she would be his love forever. Gail had her man! Their hearts burst with happiness. The two young adults were so much in love that they never stopped to think about their family's reactions when they got home. When they returned, their dreams were shattered and her young heart was broken!

Max's grandmother, one of the wealthiest and most powerful women in the county had filed proceedings to have their marriage annulled. She found out about her grandson's elopement to a 13-year-old girl from the wrong side of the social railroad tracks. She forbade Maxwell to ever see Gail again. It was over, almost as fast as it began! Gail had just found out what society thought of being the daughter of a dirt farmer. She found out that people in town felt she was "the wrong kind of people" and was labeled "too poor and uneducated" for the Jackson family. Gail's short love affair and brief marriage became an important lesson for her.

She would never forget the love she felt for Max Jackson, the second true love of her life. Nor, would she ever forget the pain.

Chapter Four

After the Annulment

MAXWELL JACKSON WOULD NOT BE easy to forget. After all, he was the love of her 13-year old life. But, Gail had been raised to be tough. She would not let this keep her from going on with her life. She continued to date other men. She loved to party, and she loved to dance. But, nothing and no one ever compared to Max. She often found herself singing the old Kitty Wells' song, *"I can't help it if I'm still in Love with You!"* She had to keep herself sane. There was still too much work to do and her daddy relied on her more and more to help it get done.

Times continued to get harder for Lloyd and Annie Mae. With Calvin now married and away in the Navy, there were still seven kids at home to feed and clothe. Gail greatly missed her brother and strongly wished for his return home. Her sisters were getting old enough now to want nice clothes and had started caring what they "looked like". Gail realized it would be up to her to help make some money. She soon found a way to make some "fast cash".

All day long, she would work in the tomato fields and as soon as she could every evening, she would sneak out and hitch a ride to the honky-tonk down the road. Gail, still so very young, with a body that concealed her age, would dance as hard as she could, occasionally stopping to have a drink and a smoke with one of the local men at the bar. She became friendly with all the men in the place but always seemed to end up hanging out with one man in particular.

His name was James Monroe, known to everyone as Jimbo. He was the "cats meow" to Gail. Jimbo always had money, and was always willing to provide her with a cigarette and drink when she got there. Eventually, she came to trust him, and soon she was describing to him how tough life was for her daddy and mama. She described the long days in the tomato fields and opened up about her wish that she could help her family make ends meet. Jimbo had the perfect solution.

He and some other guys had a very lucrative business and he asked her if she wanted to help them out for some spending money. He knew her family well. He knew the tomato fields, and the woods out behind the land her daddy owned. That is where he and his friends operated their business. They were using those woods to make moonshine. Since this was just after the depression, and prohibition was enforced, they had many requests for their product. So many, in fact, they couldn't fill all the orders because they had to be careful of the local authorities. They already had several narrow escapes, and they needed someone to be their "spotter". She had the guts to give it a try!

Against her parent's wishes, she became a spotter for Jimbo and the boys. For the next few years, she drove a brand new Ford Coupe and she tore up the roads making sure the path was clear for the liquor haulers following behind her. She knew it was wrong, but she was determined to help her mama and daddy out. Gail did this for a long time, and was good at it. She knew she was asking for trouble, but she kept thinking about her daddy and mama and how she was helping to provide for all the kids they had.

As times continued to get tough, Gail got tougher with them. She worked hard, she played hard, and she just kept searching for happiness. She felt like she would never get over Max. That's when a man caught her eye. His name was Walter Payton Sanders. He was about nine years her senior, and he reminded her so much of Max with his dark eyes, and his dark wavy hair. He had actually grown up a few miles down the road from Gail and her family, but she hadn't seen him in a long while.

Payton was at the honky-tonk with Jimbo and the boys one night when Gail walked in. He recognized her from so long ago, but couldn't believe how she had matured since the last time he had seen her. He was immediately taken by her honest and capricious personality as well as her charm. He found himself attracted to Gail physically, but soon his heart began to stir whenever she was around. He thought about her when she wasn't there, and it wasn't long before Payton took her "under his wing" so to speak. Gail felt protected by this older man. She respected his wisdom greatly. His friendship began to fill the void of loneliness and pain left by her first love. When she was around Payton, she felt safe. She knew he cared very deeply about her. In fact, she came to believe he truly loved her. The problem was, could she love him?

She could not forget the times she had spent in the arms of Max, or the memory of the burning desire that filled her soul for him. Would she still harbor those memories? Could time be kind to her and let her forget? Finally, she gave in to her feminine desires, and took Payton into her embrace. She felt his love and his respect. She felt she had found the man who would love her for who she was and thought she could love him back. Payton and Gail were happy. She had the best of it all. A loving man and the chance to do what she loved best. He took her to the honky-tonk and she danced!

Gail thought she had finally gotten over Max Jackson. That is, until the night he came back into her life. She was out one night at a local bar and ran right into Max Jackson drinking with some friends. The second their eyes met, the fire in their souls ignited once more, and every feeling they had suppressed since the annulment flooded to the surface all over again. Seeing her there with another man made his blood boil with jealousy. He still wanted her and she still wanted him. Even though his family had made it abundantly clear that he was not to see her again, Max couldn't let go. He would sneak around to see Gail under the cloak of darkness. For the longest time, Gail would lead a double life!

In her own way, she honestly did love Payton, but Max treated her like a princess. He was so good to her! She tried to refuse Max, but every time she saw him, she just couldn't stop the feelings she had for him. He had been her first, no, second, true love and he was forever burned in her heart. She would spend the days working the tomato fields and she would make as much time for Payton as she could, but she looked so very forward to the nights when she and Max would slip off together and anoint the love they felt for each other.

Chapter Five
The Baby

THE SECRET LIFE SHE WAS leading soon came to an end. In January of 1940, she had just turned 18, and she found herself pregnant! She had missed her period and was panic stricken! Surely to God, she couldn't be pregnant! Her daddy would kill her for embarrassing the family even more than she already had! In those days, it was a sin and a disgrace to be pregnant and have a baby without being married! She definitely was pregnant, and she most definitely was not married! To make matters even worse, her double life had given her two possible fathers. Payton was so very strong. He loved her very much and he would always provide for her. On the other hand, she had always been madly in love with Max. Max had always said he loved her, but, because of his family, had only loved "secretly". How could she tell Payton about her relationship with Max? How could she face the two men in her life and tell them she was pregnant- but wasn't sure which of them was the father? If Max was the father, would he accept her and her infant child? If Payton was the father, could he ever forgive her for lying to him and cheating on him? Surely, God would strike her down for this.

Mama Mae had raised her right out of the Bible. She knew she'd been taught better than this. She knew seeing two men and sleeping with them both was just plain wrong but she just couldn't stop herself. It was as if she was driven to do it. Something within her compelled her wanting to have a good time. She craved attention. She absolutely HAD to dance, and was happiest when she was smoking her filter less Lucky Strikes and drinking with the boys. So, she decided not to tell anyone. She would keep it a secret until she couldn't hide it anymore.

She continued to see Payton and Max both until she could no longer hide the pregnancy. The time came to decide whom she would tell first. She thought about them both, and decided to follow her heart. She chose to tell Max first. She was shocked when he refused to believe it was his. She always thought Max truly loved her. It wasn't until his reaction that very moment that she realized he didn't love *her* at all. Instead, He loved her *body*. The love she thought she saw was mere lust. Her first love denied her. This was Gods punishment! She was crushed!

There was only one possible solution: she had to tell Payton the truth. She would have to tell Payton about the baby, as well as the truth about Maxwell Jackson. *"If he truly loves me"*, she thought, *"he will HAVE to forgive me!"* She told Payton the whole story about her love affair with Max. She told him all about the reaction they had gotten from both of their families. She went into detail about the love they truly thought they had for each other. She wanted so badly for him to believe what she was saying and she hoped so desperately that his reaction would be one of softhearted understanding. She wanted so much for him to forgive her actions and somewhere in her efforts to make Payton care for her enough to still love her, she actually began to convince herself. Maybe she, in fact, did love Payton. She truly wanted to believe her actions to be justified and she became more determined of the outcome of her story. She even convinced herself that Payton would even accept being the father of the baby! Finally, she told Payton she was pregnant. Payton's reaction was not at all what she had expected. He took it very badly in deed!

He had trusted Gail without question. He had never even considered that she would be unfaithful. He felt like his world was exploding around him! His heart was racing quickly and his first impulse was to find Max Jackson and pulverize his slimy flesh beneath his feet. He wanted to hurt Max even worse than Max had hurt Gail. He told her he needed some time to think about it all. He honestly didn't know if he would or even *could* forgive her. Torn apart inside, he told her that maybe time would make a difference. He just wanted to get away for a while to think. He made her no promises about the outcome. Payton just went numb all over. He ended up just walking away, leaving Gail all alone, back at home once again, and pregnant!

Her fate was decided; she had made her bed, and now it was time to lay in it. The next few months were a mental agony for Gail. As the time dragged by the entire time was spent with the question of who the father was. Gail eventually gave birth to a baby girl. On October 23, 1940, Addy Mae was born to Gail Leighann Sanders, an unwed mother living on Flat Shoals Road in College Park, Georgia. Gail had to put her real address and marital status on the birth certificate, but not knowing what else to do, and to save her family from further humiliation, she placed the name "Sanders" down in the last name section of the document. It was killing her inside. Little Addy Mae had deep toned skin and dark curly hair, and Gail believed that she looked just like Max Jackson. She couldn't help but anguish over the chances that her baby belonged to him. She wondered if Max would love and accept this baby if he saw her? Gail had to know one way or the other. Besides, her baby deserved a daddy.

She wrote Max a letter and asked him to come to see her as quickly as he could. She waited nervously, and within a few weeks, he finally came to visit. She was so sure he would fall head over heals in love with Addy Mae that she wasn't prepared for the reaction. Once again, he became furious and shouted at her over and over. *"WHY DID YOU SEND FOR ME? HUH? TO SHOW ME THIS BABY?! I ALREADY TOLD YOU, GAIL MARTIN, ITS NOT MINE! YOU'RE CRAZY IF YOU THINK YOU ARE GOING TO GET ANY HELP OUT OF ME!"* Once again, he left. This time it was forever and it just about finished Gail off. All the love she thought she had for him came crashing down around her with a thunder that shook her very soul. His vehement denial of the baby she so hoped he would accept as his crushed every bit of hope in her heart. The passion she had for him instantly turned to hurt, then remorse, then just as quickly turned to anger and hatred. There was nothing else to do. She had gambled on Max twice and lost both times.

Addy Mae was just a couple of months old when brother Calvin's wife Elizabeth, otherwise known as "Lizzy", came to visit and see the baby. Lizzy could not believe what she saw. Addy Mae was the prettiest little girl she had ever seen. Her fingers were closed in tight little fists. She had one of those miniature hands stretched way behind her ear, and her tiny little mouth was chewing on the other. Her deep toned skin was so smooth you couldn't help but want to touch it. The head full of dark, curly hair stuck out from under the home made quilt Gail had her wrapped up in. Gail had finally decided she was proud of her beautiful little girl and began to hold her head high again. She didn't care what people thought.

Their dirty words would never hurt her. The new mom was trying her best to learn to be a good mother, but her mind kept wandering back to the question of the baby's father. She knew it was over with Max. She realized that much. She couldn't take any more humiliation from him. So, she set her mind on Payton. The wheels in her mind started turning and soon she was working on a plan to get Payton back. Even though Payton walked away from Gail the day she told him she was pregnant, he was never very far from her. He had loved her from the moment he had laid eyes on her. He had been there for her so many times since they met, and his being away from her found him thinking about her more and more. Watching her fiery spirit, her pride, and her headstrong determination to hold her head up despite her current situation, Payton realized that he truly wanted to be with her the rest of his life. He finally caved in from his decision to stay away and went to see her. She got her man back, and for a brief time, she had all she had hoped for. She began to see more and more of Payton and now, to Gail, her life was perfect. However, life with a baby tied her down, hindered her fun, and little Addy Mae seemed to cry more and more each day. She tried her best to balance motherhood and her womanly desires, but since Payton never accepted little Addy Mae as his, many times, the baby was left with Mama Mae and Pappy Lloyd.

Her perfect life didn't last very long. Addy Mae Sanders was taken to Egleston Children's hospital just outside of downtown Atlanta where she was pronounced dead shortly after Gail and Payton were reunited. The cause was listed as "toxemia". It was reportedly due to a stomach rupture from the bicarbonate of soda that was given to her for an upset stomach.

No one is sure how it happened. Was it an accidental overdose from an inexperienced young mother who thought she was doing the right thing? After all, she had seen her mother give a dose of bicarbonate of soda to children all her life for upset stomach. Or was it intentional? Did Gail just get tired of being tied down to a baby that had become an albatross around her neck? Had she decided that her life with Payton was worth more than the little life that she had created in her carefree sexual exploitations of her hormonal adolescents? Could it be possible that both scenarios were true to some extent? Had this young woman, who had tasted being a grown up, with all the perks and frivolities of human relations thought about her predicament and decided to "accidentally on purpose" give this little 3 month old life back to

God? For over 50 years, this unanswered question has loomed in the minds of all involved. Whatever the case was, Gail carried it to her death in February 2001.

Chapter Six

The First Few Years

When Gail turned to Payton after the death of Addy Mae and pledged her undying love to him, he wanted so much to believe it. But, there were still questions, doubts and fears in his mind. WOULD she be faithful? *COULD* she be faithful? Would she give him all her heart and soul? Would there be another Max Jackson? It was a chance he was willing to take. On November 23, 1943, Gail Leighann Martin was married to Walter Payton Sanders at a Justice of the Peace in Fulton County, Georgia. Payton purchased a few acres of land across the road from Pappy Lloyd and Mama Mae.

Payton, along with Pappy Lloyd and Gail's two brothers, Stan and Brother, built Gail a little white house in the middle of a tuft of trees. The house sat high off the ground and the steps were seemingly even higher off the ground. There were five rooms- two bedrooms, a living room/dining area separated from the kitchen by a ½ bar on one end, and a bathroom. The kitchen had a window overlooking the front yard. Payton made sure Gail's house had very nice furniture and Gail finally had the pretty lace curtains she had always liked and wanted so badly. They always had nice things to wear, and Gail soon spent much of her time in the kitchen, where she became an excellent cook. Payton, the provider Gail always knew he would be, had given up moonshine and landed a good paying job as a pipe fitter. He worked very hard to make sure Gail had the nice things he promised she would have, and to the outside world to see, she seemed truly happy.

In fact, during the first year of their marriage, Gail found herself pregnant. Thirteen months after they were married, they were expecting "their" first child. On September 19, 1945, Gail gave birth to a beautiful baby girl. They named her Patricia Leighann Sanders, and she was just as pretty as Gail's first baby. When Payton looked at this precious little baby, his first child, and she immediately became nicknamed *"Patti Cake"*, the new love of Payton's life. She was pretty as a picture. Her head was full of curly hair, and she had the most perfect skin, the most precious thing he had ever seen. Patti Cake was truly his pride and joy. With the birth of this little baby, life for Gail and Payton truly WAS perfect.

Payton became more and more content with life as time went by but he found himself wondering if Gail was adjusting to things. Was Payton just kidding himself that things were fine? Had she forgotten Max Jackson? Was there anything missing? Was he over that lack of trust he had when first taking Gail to be his bride or was he perhaps just being paranoid? Maybe things were fine.

For the next two years, Payton, Gail and Patti Cake were beautifully content. Payton loved his wife and little girl so very much. To the outside world, they had it all, and nothing seemed at all out of place in their relationship. Since they lived across the road from Gail's daddy and mama, her large family of brothers, sisters, nieces and nephews alike would spend many days together visiting and sharing dinners together. Often times you could find the families enjoying themselves outside sitting around an old black pot of hot grease frying pork skins or making chitterlings. Gail would listen to music on the radio Payton bought for her and she would hold little Patti Cake while she rocked back and forth in the old rocking chair that sat in the living room across from the old wooden stove in the corner. All the while, she would day dream about the days she used to go dancing.

Yes, everything appeared perfect and soon the happy trio found themselves about to be a foursome. Maria Diane Sanders was born on January 9, 1948. She was born a bit earlier than anticipated and she had to be taken care of very carefully. Due to her small size, feeding her was done through an Eyedropper while she was held in the palm of one hand. That didn't stop her daddy from loving her. She was given the nickname *"Dottie Bug"*.

Patti Cake and Dottie Bug filled Payton's heart with pride! One year, Patti Cake was given a rusty old tricycle. She spent hours riding her little bike up and down the dirt driveway of their house on Flat Shoals Road. One day, her little tricycle was missing and little Patti Cake was crushed. She looked all over for her little bike, including the tall wheat grass in the fields next to the house. Later that year, at Christmas, she woke up to find her little tricycle under the tree. It had been painted bright red and looked brand new! She could not believe how lucky she was to be so loved!

In later years, Payton's mother, Martha Jean Sanders, would tell them how proud he was to have two such beautiful daughters, and how he truly loved them! Payton continued to work very hard to make sure his "three girls" were provided for. Gail didn't have a job. Instead, she stayed home and took care of the babies. Most times, she was happy, and could not ask for more in life, but *sometimes*, she would get down, or a little depressed because *sometimes*, she found herself looking back at her younger days and wanting more out of life than she had.

She slowly began to second-guess the decisions she had made, all over again. I guess you could say, she would get the HONKY TONK BLUES! Payton probably saw it in her face on those days, because his doubts and insecurities grew harder and harder to control. He loved her with all his heart, but he was growing concerned about the difference in their ages. He was so much older than her. He was content with his life, but his younger and still attractive- even sexy- wife didn't seem ready to be just a housewife. *"After all"*, he thought, *"look how we met!"* He began to not trust her and soon he began drinking frequently. The more he drank, the meaner he got.

Gail began to really question whether or not she could live with him in the condition he was putting himself into. All the time that had been invested in the relationship seemed to be turning into regret and resentment. He began to resent working while she stayed home. He was sure she was doing something wrong, but could never catch her. So, he drank more and began to stay away from the house as long as he could. He started staying out later and later. She began to feel remorse for the things she didn't have any more. She started to feel like her life was a direct conflict with what she thought she wanted and fought so hard to get all those years ago.

In the back of her mind were the choices she had made in order to finally get what she wanted. So, she got depressed. Her depression angered him more. They both felt betrayed. The passion slipped away and died, and loneliness was settling in. Their minds wandered. *"Is she faithful?" "Can I live with his drinking?" "Where does he go?" "When will he be back?" "Has she forgotten about Max Jackson?" "Will he ever get over Max Jackson?" "How long could their marriage last?"* Arguments became very regular and even longer in length. What the outside world saw as a perfect little family soon became a prison for her, and Payton eventually began resenting the very life he had been working so hard to provide for. Soon, the arguments turned into fights, and the physical damage started. Payton drank more and more, leaving Gail alone in the house with two kids, and their fighting led to more depression. Their passion-heated relationship had turned into one of oil and water.

The two precious little girls, stuck in the middle of it all, began their sad journey down the path of life. Dottie Bug's memories of life with her father and mother are vague for the most part because she was only 2 years old when the memories came to an abrupt stop. Patti Cake remembers a little more because she was a few years older. However, many of Patti Cake's memories are faint flashes that children tend to block out and WANT to forget.

Life in this "perfect" little family took a major turn for the worse. The drinking and fighting had gone way beyond normal healthy spats and had turned to pure hardened and bitter anger towards each other. One night, Payton came home drunk to find Gail feeding Patti Cake at the little table in the kitchen. Words passed between the two about his drinking so much. Payton decided he didn't like what she had fixed for dinner so he grabbed the table on one end and turned it upside down. A glass of tea fell to the floor and shattered, throwing glass up into Patti Cakes eye, cutting her pretty deeply. In fact, 50 years later, the scar over her left eye is still visible.

Gail soon got tired of being scared and finally decided she needed to tell her daddy and mama about the way things were. By this time in his life, Pappy Lloyd, through his tomato farms, had a direct affiliation with several local and state government officials, direct ties to moonshine operations throughout the southeast during prohibition and had also become a very high ranking and long term member of the old South KKK. After he heard of Paytons "outbursts" towards his daughter and granddaughter, Pappy Lloyd decided to throw a little intervention party in Payton's name by arranging a cross burning in the front yard of the house that had been built for Gail. He was hoping it would warn him about hurting his daughter. Pappy Lloyds two screaming granddaughters watched the entire scene unfold while they were crying for their mother. Gail consoled her two babies and told them it was because their daddy had been mean to them and had to be taught a lesson. Once again, a 5-year old little girl and a 2-year old baby were expected to understand and accept what was happening. The cross did place a slight scare in Payton, and he calmed down for a short period, but he was soon drinking again, and angrier than ever.

Gail made a decision. She had grown tired of the arguing and the beatings she was taking from Payton. Now his temper had turned towards his baby girl. She knew she could not give in and give up. She decided to muster up all the strength that God had given her through the blessings of a hard working mother and father.

Chapter Seven

Ending the Violence

A volcano had been churning inside Gail for the longest time. On the late evening of April 15, 1950, it erupted. Payton left the house on foot that evening heading to a poker game with two of Gail's brothers-in-law and a couple of other locals. He decided to walk the two miles to the corner of Flat Shoals Road and Riverdale Road, in spite of how Gail felt about his going. Gail put the girls to bed like normal and sat alone for hours waiting and wondering what she should do.

She decided she couldn't take it any more. Gail already knew that when he came home, he would be drunk, definitely mean, and probably wanting to "play rough". She couldn't do it anymore! Her life had to change! *"Tonight, the disrespect ends!"* she promised herself. *"Tonight, I teach his ass a lesson! After tonight, there won't be any more playing cards with his buddies and God only knows what else he stays involved in!"* She made up her mind to be ready for him as soon as he walked into the kitchen door. *"I have warned him I couldn't take it any more, and now I am not playing!"*

Shortly after midnight, she heard him coming up the steps to the kitchen door. She had already planned her work, and now it was time to work her plan. From the dish drainer next to the sink, she grabbed the big cast iron skillet she had so often used to fry chicken. Her adrenaline was flowing so quickly that she picked up the heavy pan like it was nothing. She stood on the chair behind the door, waiting for him to come staggering into the kitchen as he had so many times in the past. *"The bastard's going to be sorry he left me here alone again and even sorrier if he's drunk!"* As the door opened slowly, and Payton stepped into the kitchen, without looking at him or giving him time to open his mouth, Gail swung that old black frying pan over her head as hard as she could. Her aim was sure and the pan hit him hard, directly in the back of his head. Payton fell to the floor hard, never once flinching.

She just stood there in the chair, both fists clenching the frying pan. She was waiting for his next move. She was so sure Payton was going to retaliate and this would end up in a long night of fighting. She was prepared for it. She was protecting herself and her babies and the man who had finally broken her patience was not going to break her spirit.

She stood there in that chair a second or two longer. He didn't move a muscle. Blood was beginning to puddle on the floor around his head. After she regained her composure, she could see that he had already been in a fight. There was a big red bruise on the side of his face that she knew she hadn't done. Suddenly, she realized he was seriously hurt. The pan she had been holding in her hand became so heavy in her arms that she dropped it. She panicked. What had she done? What should she do? Her mind was racing and her thoughts turned to the frying pan she had just had in her hands. She quickly picked it up, and almost unconsciously rinsed it off and put it back in the dish drainer she had just pulled it from. As fast as she could, she ran out of the house screaming. She ran across the street to her mama and daddy's house to get help. Pappy Lloyd came across the road to investigate what had happened.

Mama Mae followed behind her husband almost dragging a crying and reluctant Gail by her left arm. Pappy Lloyd gathered Payton up. He carried the docile large framed man across the road to his old pick up truck.

Payton was taken to Crawford Long Hospital in Downtown Atlanta, not far from the place Payton and Gail had been married barely 5 years ago. The emergency room took him in, admitted him and diagnosed him as being in a coma in critical condition. Gail was hysterical! *"What have I done?"* She could not calm down. *"What if he dies? What will happen to my beautiful little babies?"* She begged God to help her. *"Please let Payton LIVE!"* All of a sudden, Gail started thinking about the situation. She thought about how she had purposely climbed in the chair behind the door. She remembered the feeling of malicious intent to harm him. She had promised herself to teach him a lesson. Memories of his beatings and his verbal abuse flooded her mind. She remembered the cut above little Patti Cake's eye and she became numb as an even more sinister thought came over her. *"What if he lives? What then? Which would be worse? Living with his drinking, or living with the thought that I may have killed him."*

Now she was really in a bind. All she could do is wait, and try to keep her mind off either thought. She rarely left Payton's side. The only time she was not sitting next to his bed was when the nurses would make her leave so they could change the bandages. She sat vigil over him, as a good wife should. For nine days she waited, grateful that her mother and her sisters were taking turns caring for her two babies.

The last night Payton was alive, Gail's sister, Ellie Stills, and her husband Alan had come to sit with Gail. They saw how tired she was, and asked her when last she had eaten anything. Gail couldn't remember. In fact, she was sure it had been days ago. She just couldn't leave his side. Everyone thought she was being a doting wife. They had no clue of the real reason. No one could have guessed it was because she was tormented inside trying not to think about the night she may have killed her husband. Alan gave Gail a couple of dollars and told her to go down the hall to the vending area in the cafeteria. They would watch Payton for her and promised to come and get her if anything changed. She had just sat down in the cafeteria to smoke a cigarette, drink an RC Cola and eat the Moon Pie she had bought with the money she was given. Ellie came running into the cafeteria crying. *"Gail, you need to come back to the room. Payton's just died."*

Walter Payton Sanders died on April 24, 1950 at the age of 36. His 2-year old daughter Maria Diane Sanders, his 5-year old daughter Patricia Leighann Sanders, and a beautiful, still desirable 28-year old woman named Gail Leighann Sanders survived him. His mother, Martha Jean Sanders, faced an unnatural situation. A parent is not supposed to bury the child. The child is supposed to bury the parent. She was sure Payton's mother would not accept his death easily. Gail was not sure what the outcome would be, but in her most vivid fears, she could never have prepared herself for the events to follow in the days ahead.

There was a lot of paperwork to sign at the hospital then Ellie and Alan took Gail by her parents home to pick up Patti Cake & Dottie Bug. She was so tired and the stress of Payton's death left her drained. She wanted to see her two baby girls. She had thought so much about them for the past week while she sat and watched Payton's chest rise and fall with the shallow breaths he took. It wasn't the first time she had been downtown, but that ride home turned out to be the longest ride she had ever been on. She thought they would never get there. She hugged her mama, thanked her for watching the kids, then took her sleeping babies home, just across the road.

The house was unusually quiet. She kept her two little girls next to her all night. They never left her. She felt safe and that was a feeling she hadn't felt in so long. She drifted to sleep wondering just how she would tell Patti Cake and Dottie Bug their daddy was dead. Tomorrow would turn out to be a big day- bigger than she was ready for. She got up early the next morning to make breakfast. She fed the girls and decided it was time for them to know about the daddy they loved so much. Dottie Bug was still so young, she didn't know what was happening. All Patti Cake understood is that her daddy had gone away, and she missed him. She wanted him back.

While her daughter sat at the window, sad and missing her daddy, Gail stood in the kitchen, helpless to explain it any better than she had. She was staring out the kitchen window looking out into the front yard and driveway. Patti Cake was staring out the living room window. They both saw the silver police cruiser pull up in the front yard and drive up to the front door. It was strange to little Patti Cake, because when company visited, they always parked around back and came in the back door. She got scared and ran to her mother in the kitchen, grabbing her mama's pants leg as the front door was knocked on. Gail's heart sank and her throat closed up. She was afraid to breathe. Her mind was flooded with thoughts of her babies. Tears immediately streamed down her cheeks. She knew what was happening. She had anticipated it. She knew that Payton's mom was upset, and she fully expected some type of reaction, but this was so quick. It was all happening so quickly. Gail had her oldest child attached to her leg as she opened the door. He was a very big man, much taller than Gail, especially to a frightened five-year-old girl. He walked into the living room and began talking to Gail. Patti Cake could not understand the conversation but the look on her mama's face frightened her. She was crying deeply and soon little Dottie Bug was crying, too.

Gail and the big man talked a few more minutes and then Gail started getting her two little babies ready to go for a ride.

While she was getting Patti Cake dressed she was saying, *"You're going to visit with Granny Sanders. Won't you like that? I want you to be a big girl, and help Granny Sanders with your baby sister. I will be back for you soon. Don't be scared, its ok. I just need to go with this man for a little while."* Soon, the three of them were escorted into the back seat of the car. The house was locked and they drove off.

The car stopped outside of Martha Jean's house where Patti Cake and Dottie Bug were greeted by their grandmother and their daddy's sister-in-law. Her name was Florence Jean Sanders, known to the little girls as "Aunt Flo". She was glad to help out in anyway she could. Gail kissed her babies good bye. She was crying as she promised them she would be back soon. Aunt Flo and Granny Sanders took the girls in the house and the big man drove off in the silver police car with Gail in the back of it.

Two days later, it was time for Payton's funeral. Dottie Bug and Patti Cake were dressed in pretty little outfits that Granny Sanders had bought for them. Payton was brought to his mama's house at 119 Tanner Road in College Park for the wake. The furniture in the big family room had all been cleared out. The large, rectangular room was filled mostly with people standing around. The coffin was in one corner and a few flower arrangements were lining the walls. Family members and people from all over the area were there. Patti Cake was standing beside her daddy's coffin when her Aunt Flo picked her up and told her to say good bye to her daddy. Patti Cake did what she was told, but she still didn't realize that she would never see her daddy again.

As the days passed, Granny Sanders did all she could to make the little girls feel at home. To the girls, Granny Sanders seemed to be rich. Her house was so nice! It was so much bigger than the house the girls were used to living in. There was real tile in the bathroom that sparkled like diamonds. The house always smelled as if a feast was cooking in her large kitchen. Years later, the smell of apple pie cooking still brings back such fond memories.

The large chain linked fence in the back yard was there to protect the prettiest green grass they had ever seen, and Patti Cake and Dottie Bug would love nothing better than to walk up and down the sidewalk in front of the house. They played games like "Step on a Crack". Just around the corner from Granny Sanders house was Nealy Grammer School and the huge cement area in the playground where Patti Cake would skate for hours. Around and around she would skate, pretending she was a movie star. Neither of them remembered who gave them their first skates, but skating became their passion. A passion that somehow made up for never having been on a vacation with their mother.

Each afternoon, Granny Sanders would lay them down for their nap in the front bedroom the house on the softest bed they ever felt. They were growing to love this life so much. Many times, Granny Sanders would dress Patti Cake and Dottie Bug and they would take walks to the neighbor's house to visit. They always enjoyed walking with their grandma and they would pick handfuls of flowers from the large flowerbeds that lined her yard.

After a few months, they woke up from their nap to find their mama sitting in the den with their grandmother and a few other people. They were both so excited to see her! They ran to her open arms, screaming *"MAMA! MAMA!"* Gail cried while she held her two little babies in her arms. She had been away for so long. She had thought about her babies the whole time she was away and Gail vowed that very second that no one would ever separate her from her children again! She would provide for her babies, regardless of how she had to do it.

Chapter Eight

A New Life

EVEN THOUGH PATTI CAKE AND DOTTIE BUG enjoyed living with their Granny Sanders immensely, they had both missed their mama and were glad to be going home with her, thinking they were going back to the home their daddy built for them. Instead, Gail took them to 104 South Lee Street, in College Park, to a house much older and not nearly as nice as what the little girls were accustomed to living in. Payton's life insurance had landed Gail enough money to pay down on a small home for her and her daughters. Years earlier whoever started the construction on the home had simply quit working on the house and it had since aged badly. It was constructed similar to the house they had known, with two medium sized bedrooms, a small bathroom, a kitchen, and a living room. There was no comparing the condition of this house to the one that Payton had built for Gail shortly after they were married. Still, she was determined to make the best of her current situation and felt sure she could one day make it a good home for her and her daughters.

On the outside of the house was a very ugly gray asbestos siding. The plain, gray house had no shutters to decorate the windows. There was no carport or garage. The yards were unkempt, untamed, and large patches of weeds grew inside the crabgrass that sparsely dotted a yard that had, most likely, never saw a lawnmower. Near the street the yard was a mushy mess where stood the dark smelly waters of an overflowing septic line. Apparently, "curb appeal" was never a priority in this yard.

The house was perched at the top of a hill, the land long and narrow with an upward slope. The plain dirt driveway sat six or eight steps away from unpainted and barely stacked concrete blocks leading up several feet to a screened in front porch. Over the years, holes ripped into those screens leaving little indication that the wooden frames were covered with screens at all.

On the way to the front door, visitors had to carefully step over several rotted or missing boards. Visible through those loose and missing planks was a large hole in the ground that had apparently started out to be a basement before the owner of the house abandoned efforts to complete the construction. The two girls had very active imaginations and their creative minds conjured visions of the Boogieman standing and waiting for them to cross over the porch. They had talked themselves into being very afraid and always leery of walking over those ominous holes.

There was no central air conditioning or heat; instead, only a small heater stood in the living room to provide warmth for them during the cold winter months. The previous owner had painted the plain, hard wood floors all through the house except in the living room. There the floor was covered by a linoleum rug that showed signs of wear and fading with time. The curtains that hung in the living room were fiberglass drapes that Gail bought and hung on some cheap white rods. Half of the curtain rings were missing and the way the curtains hung so loosely from the rods, it looked as if they would fall to the floor at any time.

There was nothing at all fancy in the house and it was obvious that Gail furnished 104 South Lee Street with hand-me-downs and mismatched pieces. The bathroom was dark and dirty looking, with bare floors and walls. Next to the soap dish was a hole so large that Dottie Bug and Patti Cake could actually see through to the ground!

In the kitchen, there were no built in appliances or other "modern" conveniences. There was only a plain white sink with white, single-cabinets with no doors hung on either side. The hot water heater stood in the corner between the cooking stove and a door that led to the back porch and down 10 or so feet to a long, narrow side yard. It was in that side yard where Gail used to hang wet clothes on an old pig wire fence belonging to the Smiths.

Neither of the girls could remember when their mother started working but Gail had a job at Stocktons Metal Works welding wrought iron. She would come home each afternoon, almost solid black, soot covering everything from head to toe, with just the large circles around her eyes that were covered with her goggles. Since she worked during the week, Gail had a hired a young black woman to watch her little girls during the day. The young girl didn't communicate with the two girls very much so neither of them missed her after Gail caught her stealing and made her leave the house. Shortly afterwards, Gail hired an older woman named Jewel to sit with them. Jewel was always good to the young girls and they both enjoyed sitting on the front steps combing through Jewel's long, black Cherokee Indian hair. The two of them were amazed that her hair went all the way down her back to her waist!

Neither Dottie Bug nor Patti Cake have many good memories of the time they spent at this house, but perhaps the best memory they do have, and one of the few times they reflect on with a smile, is the rare occasions when the house was filled with the sweet smell of those amazing teacakes their mama used to make. Even as grown women, they can almost smell the sweet, mouth-watering aroma that lingered like a bakery in that horrid little house!

Another prominent memory is the mandatory visits every week to Sunday school. Every Sunday Gail packed her babies up and drove down to her sister Annie's house where they would pick her and her children up and head to Pleasant Grove Methodist church, later known as Riverdale Methodist Church, on Riverdale Road. The original old Church is gone now, but the adjacent cemetery is still there, and that is where most of Patti Cake and Dottie Bugs family is buried, including their daddy, Walter Payton Sanders and the would-be older sister that passed away as an infant, Addie Mae Sanders. Sadly, until recently, Walter and Addie Mae had only plain bread pan sized pieces of concrete marking their graves. (But we will get to that later.) They both remember how intent the services were back then, and how, like children often do, they would get restless and start squirming. How that squeeze on the hand would settle them down!

Other than the few memories they can muster up, both of them remember how often they would walk the really short distance to their Granny Sanders house. Patti Cake would drag little Dottie Bug behind her many times over the next periods of their lives.

Chapter Nine

The Man at the Drive-In

NEITHER OF THE LITTLE GIRLS can remember their mama crying much during those years after their daddy died. Perhaps it was because they stayed with their Granny Sanders so much of the time. Perhaps she would cry when she was away from the girls. Maybe she just wanted to be strong for her babies. In any case, she seemed to move on with her life.

Gail was, after all, a young woman. Though she had been widowed at 28, she was still in the prime of her life and still had needs as a woman. Those oh-so-strong urges that got her in trouble when she was young were beginning to surface again. It had not been so long since she had them, but to her, it had been too long since she acted upon them.

One day, a Dutch Oven bread truck drove up in the driveway of the man next door. However, when the driver got out, he came knocking on Gail's door instead. It had to have been summer time, because Patti Cake and Dottie Bug were playing outside. The driver knocked on the door and Gail let him in. When

Patti Cake tried to go in the house after him, but she was told to stay outside for a while and play with Dottie Bug. In effort to "make it ok" for them to stay outside, the "Bread Man" went to his truck and got two chocolate éclairs for Gail to give her little girls. To this day, they both laugh when they remember the "Dutch Oven Man". It was most likely the first man Gail had an affair with after her husbands death.

Patti Cake was about to turn 8 years old and Dottie Bug was five, not much more than a baby the night Gail put them in the car and they drove to Roosevelt Highway just outside of College Park to a diner that offered curb service. It was more like a beer joint, with the neon lights flickering on and off outside the small little building. Gail ordered them a burger and fries and when the waitress brought the food, it was the biggest burger either of the girls had ever seen. Since it was their first trip to a restaurant, both of them were so happy to get it!

A few cars down the row a man kept looking over at Gail. Gail already knew him. His name was John Louis Wyatt, Payton's first cousin. Gail knew him as Johnny. He sauntered down to Gail's car and stood on the passenger side, very close to where Patti Cake was sitting. He leaned down and into the window and started talking to Gail. Even though he was obviously a lot younger, Gail still had her sexy looks and this handsome young man caught her eye, too. After a few minutes of talking through the window, Patti Cake was told to get in the back seat and Johnny climbed into the passenger seat. Whatever the conversation was, Johnny made his way back home with Gail that night, and ended up staying with Gail every night from then on. He would get up very early and go to work at Delta Airlines then come by for dinner each evening.

Johnny seemed to like Gail's two girls, but they didn't care much for him. He interfered with their life with their mom. She started acting almost as if she cared more for "him" than she cared about her flesh and blood. Six weeks later on September 22, 1953, just 3 days after Patti Cake turned 8, Gail and Johnny became "Mr. and Mrs. John Lewis Wyatt". Johnny tried to be good to the girls. They used to crawl on top of him and ride piggy back through the house.

He used to put them on his shoulders and carry them around every where. He really did care for Gail, and Gail seemed happy. Her daughters wanted so much for her to be happy, therefore they would try their best to stay out of the way and not interrupt life with Johnny. The two of them laughed a lot, and the sex life was great! It had to have been, because Patti Cake and

Dottie Bug spent many, many hours playing outside, just like when the "Dutch Oven Man" would visit.

Using sheer imagination and their love for each other, they would create their own little home from left over cement blocks. They had a pretend refrigerator, their own little pretend sink and a pretend stove. Gail gave them some jar lids and some spoons so they would have "dishes" and they would go make believe "grocery shopping" and pick up rocks and sticks and leaves for food. Neither of the children had many friends, so they occupied their time together. They played as if they were the only two people in the world.

Meanwhile, the little girls wore hand-me-downs or home made skirts and blouses. They looked poor as church mice. Yet, the only time either of them knew they were different was the day Patti Cake got the opportunity to visit her friend Angela Sherron. Her house was so warm and cozy and, oh, it smelled so clean! Patti Cake was sure Angela was rich because she had orange juice to drink. Angela's little bedroom amazed Patti Cake. There were lace curtains, little pillows and pretty little dolls. That was the first time the two little girls knew they were different from the other children.

Two of the neighborhood kids they could play with were a sister and brother named Brenda Craig, who was Patti's age and Andrew Craig, who was Dottie Bug's age. Patti Cake and Dottie Bug went there almost every day, walking the one block with excitement and anticipation. Mr. Craig had built a giant swing set in their back yard for all of the kids to play on, and while Dottie Bug and Andrew would pretend to be the audience, Brenda and Patti Cake would pretend to be famous trapeze artists by swinging their legs wildly and doing what tricks they knew.

Gail and Johnny rarely ever called the girls home and Mrs. Craig often provided lunch and even dinner while Patti Cake and Dottie Bug were 'staying out of the way'. Mr. and Mrs. Craig never minded the children playing there, but sometimes, Mrs. Craig would have to tell the children it was too late to play and send them home. Sadly, Patti Cake would escort Dottie Bug back to the reality that was happening at 104 South Lee Street.

Gail and Johnny were in love and Gail spent much of her time taking care of his needs. In fact, taking care of Johnny seemed to have become her reason for living, consuming more and more of her time until she soon began to slight her own little girls needs. She would take him to work every day, regardless of what shift he was working. His shifts varied from week to week, sometimes working mornings, sometimes afternoons, and even some mid night shifts. Regardless, Gail was in her car several times a day driving to and from the Atlanta Airport. She loved him so much Johnny even had his lunches and dinners brought to him each day - even in the middle of the night. It didn't matter.

Gail was never big on housework. After she let Johnny move in with her and the girls, housework was the last thing on her mind. Gail thought her only job was to take care of Johnny's every desire and let the girls clean up. She lived to please him, her every desire was to make him happy. She knew she was damned lucky to have a younger man love her. She knew what he needed and what he liked and to hell with everything else.

Johnny made good money, but a lot of it was spent on liquor and cigarettes that he consumed every day. He also loved Gail's cooking and easily became used to having three home meals every day. He thought of himself as a "king" the way Gail would cook and bring his food to him hot from the kitchen. When Johnny told Gail his favorite food was shrimp, Gail quickly headed off to the store to please her man. In Gail's self-absorbed need to please Johnny, she never thought about getting enough to feed her little girls.

One of Gail's special meals for "him" was corn bread, coleslaw, pinto beans, French fries and an extra big helping of fried shrimp. She called out *"Supper is ready!"* Patti Cake, Dottie Bug and Johnny all came to the table, where the smell of fried shrimp made their mouths water. As Gail placed Johnny's plate in front of him, it was piled high with shrimp, but when the two little girls were handed their plates, there was no shrimp. *"Where is ours?"* Patti Cake asked her mother. *"There is not enough for ya'll to eat. You need to eat what is on your plate and be happy!"* The clean up of that meal and every meal to follow was given to the little girls.

Gail's kitchen had no garbage can. Instead, she and Johnny used a corner of the kitchen next to the hot water heater to throw scraps and trash in. After the garbage had piled so high they could no longer step around it to get to the stove, Johnny would tell one of the girls to rake it up and throw it outside under the back porch. He said he was growing worms and the garbage would make the dirt richer. Patti Cake and Dottie Bug would argue as to who would clean up the garbage, because there was always maggots under the trash and both of them were always afraid to touch them.

However, cleaning the maggot filled trash from the kitchen floor was nothing compared to the task of cleaning the bathroom.

Toilet paper was never bought but the little girls never knew the difference. Instead, after they went to the bathroom, they were instructed to use the old rags that Gail kept on the top of the toilet. After cleaning themselves, they were to throw the rags in a pile behind the bathroom door where the soiled rags would lay until the next time one of them did a "knocking" of clothes in the old ringer washer machine that sat in the corner of the kitchen. Johnny seemed to need more of the old rags than the girls did. Instead of sitting on the toilet like the girls, when Johnny used the bathroom, he would crawl up on the commode and squat like an Indian. He never bothered to shut the bathroom door and it seemed as though every time he used the bathroom, he would call for one of the little girls to come in and give him a rag. This was almost a ritual for him, as though he enjoyed showing his manhood to the little girls. Neither of the two little girls could understand what that *"thing"* was hanging between his legs. He just seemed to smile at them with those black eyes as if he knew of their puzzlement. The two small girls soon realized that "daddies" must be different when they "pottied" and accepted it as the way things were with Johnny.

    Patti Cake would always gag every time she had to touch those nasty rags, but when it was Dottie Bug's turn to clean the rags, she just took it in stride, thinking it was just the way life with Johnny would be.

When Johnny would get so drunk that he ended up in the bathroom vomiting, the vomit Johnny left in the sink was just as sickening. Patti Cake always wondered why he would not just turn and vomit in the commode so it could be flushed instead of having to be cleaned up from the sink, often times clogging the sink to the point that a plunger had to be used to open the drains.

Gail and Johnny's bedroom was not as bad to clean. All they had to do was empty all the cigarette butts, pick up their dirty underwear, and take the nasty whisky glasses to the kitchen. The living room barely had furniture – a ragged sofa and chair and three cheap little tables – so all they had to do was sweep the old linoleum floor, pick up nasty plates and glasses and empty the always full ashtrays. The house always smelled bad to Patti Cake. She did not know what the odor was, but it seemed to attack her when she opened the door. Patti Cake and Dottie Bug would walk home from school expecting to jump into their daily chores. But, on rare occasions, when they opened the door, they would be surprised by the sweet smell of pine clean. The smell was such a dramatic change from the stale odors that always greeted them, the wonderful sensation of pine clean never left them, even as grown women. Smells for Patti Cake and Dottie Bug were the most dramatic memories the two little girls ever remember from their childhood.

Johnny was always very jealous of Gail and did not want her to be around other men. Because he was not a religious man, after he moved in Gail quit taking her little girls to church herself. Gail, however, was a God-Fearing woman and still wanted her little girls to attend church. Though they were raised Methodist, Gail found a Baptist Church about four blocks from the house and she would send them walking by themselves to church. This would allow Gail to keep her little girls in Sunday school and still allow her to spend time with Johnny while they were gone. Patti Cake would watch over Dottie Bug and make sure she got to her class then she would stand around a while before someone would come along and direct her to her age class.

After Sunday School was over, Patti Cake would watch the crowds pour into the sanctuary for service. She would take Dottie Bug by the hand and take her in and sit down in one of the empty pews – just as her mother had done her so many times before. Neither of the little girls knew just how they stood out from the crowd. The children their own ages never had anything to do with them and the older people would look at them as if they were not supposed to be there. Patti Cake never understood a thing the preacher said, so she knew Dottie Bug was lost in the sermons. They would sit quietly together, never making a sound, until everyone got up and started to leave. They would walk down the steps together and hold hands on the way home, never talking about their experience, Sunday after Sunday. Patti Cake always hated the smell of the little Baptist Church. The smell was like the flowers that sat around the living room in her Granny Mae's home when her REAL daddy was laying there DEAD. Why couldn't their mama take them back to the little white church they had loved so much. Everyone knew them there and they had fun. Their mama was with them then and they never had to be afraid. Even the squeeze of their hands from their mama would be a welcome touch.

When Johnny was off from work, he and Gail loved to go fishing. They would pack up the old car with worms they had dug up from the worm bed by the back porch, bottles of liquor, packs of cigarettes for them, and junk food for the girls. Johnny and Gail would tell the girls to play in the sand by the creek while they went down the stream to fish. The girls always heard their mama laughing with Johnny, and then sometimes, they didn't hear anything. Patti Cake always seemed to worry. She was frightened by the woods around her and Dottie Bug and hated being left alone like they were. Gail and Johnny finally got tired of hearing them complain about their fishing trips and decided to take the girls down to Johnny's mother's house whenever they wanted to go fishing. Johnny's mother was a nice lady and they enjoyed being around her. They missed their real granny and somehow this filled an empty spot with the two girls. Mama Wyatt showed them how she picked eggs from the chickens, grew her own food and basic facts about living in the country like putting ice in the ice box and cooking on an old wood stove. Patti Cake and Dottie Bug soon learned how to use the "out house" and using the Sears and Roebuck catalog to wipe with. Mostly, things were not bad at all staying in the country. They both enjoyed that much more than spending time by a riverbed.

However, after a few months went by, something happened that scared Patti Cake half to death. Johnny's daddy walked up behind her and put his arms around her so that his hands landed on her breasts. She was so scared as she turned around and saw him standing there staring at her. He looked just like Johnny, only older. Patti Cake jumped back and started running, looking for Mama Wyatt. That was the start of many more encounters with that mean looking man and Patti Cake. Patti Cake never told her mama, but she started making excuses so that she didn't have to go back there. Her crying and screaming fits finally paid off with her mama and Johnny. Reluctantly, she was told she could stay home. Patti Cake was learning the will to survive early in her life and as the years unfolded, that inner strength would be needed again and again during her life with her mother and the man called Johnny.

Dottie Bug was still taken down to the country with Johnny's parents for the next few months, until the crying began with her as well. She didn't want to go back, either. Patti Cake never asked Dottie Bug asked why she didn't want to go back. Instead, it was as if no words were needed. Patti Cake just knew. Without a lot of fuss, Patti Cake told her mother that she would take care of her little sister while they were on their fishing trips. Almost like a relief, Gail and Johnny started leaving the two girls alone while the two of them continued to seek and find new adventures for them to be alone and in love.

Chapter Ten

All in the Family

JUST WHEN PATTI CAKE AND DOTTIE BUG thought they were unhappy and things couldn't get worse, Johnny invited his family up to visit for the weekend. A visit that turned into one of the most horrific memories either of them ever remember! His daddy, his mother, his four brothers, and his younger sister all came that weekend. Then they came the next weekend, and many weekends after. Eventually, there were additional beds scattered through out the house and they would take turns staying for weeks at a time.

The whole group would pile into cars- four adults in the front and however many kids could fit into the back. They would go to the lake and fish all day and then they would stay up all night smoking, drinking and playing cards. Where they all slept can not be remembered. All the girls can remember now is the little red chrome legged table being filled with liquor glasses and cards. They both remember being told to go to bed and not bother anyone. How could anyone expect them to sleep with all that noise going on just feet from them in the other room? The next morning, the house would be filled with Hank Williams, Sr. and other bluegrass and honky-tonk music. The two little girls were subjected to whatever the grownups wanted to listen to and never had the opportunity to watch television unless it was something the grownups wanted to watch. Yes, they had become the Georgia Hillbillies!

Soon, Gail was telling her little girls that she was going to have a baby. Patti Cake's heart filled with anger. She didn't want her mama to have a baby with their step father because a baby would take away even more of the limited amount of time her mama gave them already. As fate had it, Gail got very sick and was admitted to the hospital where she spent the next few days. She experienced complications with her pregnancy and suffered a miscarriage, losing the baby that Johnny was so proud to have produced.

However, losing the baby never deprived Johnny of her wifely duties. Very quickly, she was back to cooking for him, ironing his uniforms, and taking him back and forth to work. In the hot summers, she would set the ironing board on the front porch and stand there with nothing on but her bra and panties still making sure Johnny had a freshly pressed uniform and ready for work.

Johnny and Gail had been married for two years already. The first attempt to have a child failed, but Gail found that she was pregnant again. One month before Patti Cake turned 10 years old, Gail gave birth to Jennifer Lynn Wyatt. She came to be known as Jenny. As soon as Jenny was born, Patti Cake and Dottie Bug's life was changed forever, but life went on as usual for their mom and stepfather.

They continued to have sex, go fishing, and running up and down the road to the airport several times a day. When Jenny was 9 months old, she developed spinal meningitis. Gail and Johnny were so worried about her that when she came through it, she became their "Perfect Little Angel" and nothing she did could be wrong. She never got spankings, and never had to do any chores. To Patti Cake and Dottie Bug, she was "Perfect Spoiled Rotten" and they were both constantly subjected to her temper tantrums. When the girls got old enough, instead of dropping Jenny off with Johnny's mother while they went fishing, Patti Cake or Dottie Bug were made to baby sit her. Neither of them liked her at all and neither were able to accept her as a real sister. Partiality arose and Johnny started treating them as stepchildren are often treated.

They both felt like orphans but the worse thing that could have happened to either of them was the cancellation of visits to

Granny Sanders! As soon as Jenny was born, they were not allowed to visit their beloved grandmother at all! They had been without their daddy for five years and they both started asking questions. Each time their mama would tell them, *"Shut up! Don't let your step daddy hear you asking questions like that!"* In an attempt to rationalize with the little girls, Gail decided to tell them about their would-be older sister Addy Mae Sanders. She told them that Granny Sanders had killed her when she was born and that she was a bad person. Gail hoped this would stop them from wanting to see their grandmother. Since the little girls didn't know any better, they accepted it as truth, and for years, they believed their mothers story.

As the girls grew older, many things about their life depressed them. They purposely did not have anyone over to visit. They grew tired of living in such a dirty environment. They were deprived of a normal childhood, forced to clean walls covered with black smoke stains, grimy handprints, and greasy finger prints. They did the best cleaning jobs they knew how to do, considering their untrained capabilities. There was nothing even as simple as toilet paper in their house. When they needed to clean themselves, their mother told them to use one of the wash clothes and put it in a pile under the sink, or in the corner of the bathroom.

The house continued to age and the back steps eventually rotted and fell off. They had to make sure the back door stayed closed to keep someone from accidentally falling that long drop to the ground. The yards were always cluttered with debris blown off the streets or trash cans. The adults did not seem to care, but little Patti Cake and Dottie Bug kept to their daily chores and babysitting Jenny.

When they were young, they could still play outside, but as Patti Cake got older, she began to want to stay in the house and listen to music, or go to a friends house. She ended up leaving Dottie Bug to play alone. Once, Dottie Bug was playing at Andrew and Brenda's house. She ran home to use the bathroom and found the front door locked. She knew her mama and Johnny were home, so she walked around to the back of the house to yell for them to open the door. The window to her mama's room was wide open. What she saw that day never left her mind and it would haunt her many years later. She could not tell if he was hurting her mama, or if her mama was actually enjoying it, but she saw her mama laying there totally naked on the bed in front of the window, Johnny hovering above her, also totally naked. Dottie Bug just stood there. Her mama's eyes met hers but she never opened her mouth. Dottie Bug ran away crying, so afraid she would be in trouble for witnessing everything. Afterward, Gail never tried to talk to her about it, and most assuredly never tried to explain.

By now, Johnny had started drinking more and more and the alcohol was poisoning his outlook and his demeanor. He cursed a lot now, and what ever the reason- his job, or his home life, he cursed the world very regularly. The more he drank, the more he and Gail fought. In fact, Johnny did not waste his anger on just his wife. He was plain out mean to his stepchildren. He never missed an opportunity to pull off his belt and hit one of the girls with it. In turn, Gail and he would fight about that and soon it was just part of living there.

They were all on pins and needles all the time. It was having a negative influence on the two sweet little girls. Dottie Bug started hardening with life experiences and picking up some unpleasant habits from the grown ups they were living around. When she was in the fourth grade and it was time for school pictures, the photographer asked her if she wanted to remove her sweater because it had a hole in it. She remembers even today how she pulled the sweater close, gave him a *"Go To Hell!"* look and spoke those very words.

As soon as Johnny got off his shift at Delta Airlines, he would stop by the package store on the corner of Virginia Avenue and buy a pint of whiskey. He would drink it straight from the bottle on the way home. Dottie Bug would crawl into the floor of the back seat and pray that no one would see her. Once, Patti Cake brought home a friend of hers, Margie Weems. Margie was Patti Cakes idol! Margie had all nice clothes, shoes that matched, and she was very pretty. They had traded shoes that day in school. When Johnny came home from work and found Margie there visiting, he was furious! His very words were, *"What the hell is she doing here? Get rid of her God Damn It! I don't need this shit when I get home from work!"* Patti Cake was humiliated and wanted to die. Gail had to take Margie home. On another occasion, the family was sitting at the red and chrome-legged table having dinner. Johnny and Gail started arguing and Johnny picked up the table, spilling the contents on the girls and Gail. The fight continued and Gail ended up with a broken collarbone.

The hearts of those sweet little girls was filling with hatred. They hated Johnny altogether- his drinking, his verbal abuse, his physical abuse. They hated their life. They hated their mother for letting this continue. As Patti Cake matured, she began to realize just what her mama had been doing with Johnny behind closed doors. She hated that as well. It made her sick to think of her mother doing *"that"* with *"HIM"*. They were ashamed of themselves and the way they lived. This was how they grew up.

Chapter Eleven

A New Beginning.

For One of Them, Anyway.

LIFE WENT ON, AS THEY SAY, and by the time Patti Cake was 13, she had a lot of her mother in her. She was already filling out and she was pretty as a picture. Her outgoing personality attracted people to her almost instantly. Dottie Bug had turned to her school books for comfort, but Patti Cake turned to boys- at least one in particular. His name was Wayne Charles Coachman. She knew him as Chuck, and he didn't live far from them. She was in the 8th grade at the time and he was a junior. He was a very good looking young man that played Varsity Baseball at school. He became very taken with Patti Cake from the start. Looking back it was apparent that Patti Cake was *very* much like her mother! This greatly irritated Johnny because he had already told her she was too young to have boyfriends. Johnny took advantage of every opportunity to flaunt authority over his stepdaughters, but Patti Cake was beginning to rebel against him.

She began to spend more and more time after school visiting Chuck and was soon skipping school so she could hang out with him and his friends. Patti Cake gave Chuck her home phone number one day and when Chuck called the house looking for her, Johnny went mad with anger. After that, she stayed in trouble with Johnny. He didn't want her seeing Chuck and he would beat her with a belt when he even thought she had sneaked around and saw him at a friends house. Each time Patti Cake saw Chuck she would scream at the top of her lungs how much she hated her stepfather.

She would tell him stories about their life and Chuck would listen to every word. His own father was an alcoholic so he knew what she must be going through. His mother separated from his father many years ago because of the abuse. He remembered what it was like to be beat on as a child. He had so much sympathy for her and it made her feel so cared for and safe. She longed to be with him so much that she used to sit in the front yard in the sun hoping he would drive by and see her in her bathing suit. He would oblige, driving by several times just to see if she was there.

One afternoon, Johnny was talking down about Patti Cake and Gail said something back to him in her defense. Johnny immediately got furious and grabbed her from behind with both arms. He squeezed her so tight it broke several of her ribs. She screamed in agony. Patti Cake remembers the night like it was yesterday. Her mama was wearing a pair of dark green corduroy pants and a red Chinese print blouse. She looked so pretty! Seeing her mother in pain like that drove her to run to the kitchen, grab a big butcher knife and point the knife right at Johnny's chest. When he let her go, she fell to the floor, crying. Patti Cake told him that if he ever hurt her mama like that again she was going to kill him. That night, Patti Cake slept lightly with the butcher knife under her pillow, just in case.

It wasn't long after that Gail convinced Johnny to let Patti Cake go off with Chuck on a double date. The two of them sat for hours talking about their lives and what changes they would make. A few days later, Johnny was drinking again and getting meaner with each drink. He and Patti Cake started arguing about something again and he began to get violent with her. She picked up the phone and called Chuck to come and take her away from there. Johnny yanked the phone from her hand and slammed it down, smashing the little record player, the one she loved so dearly. Dottie Bug was scared to death! She was afraid her sister was about to be killed right in front of her. He was so mad! Chuck sped into the driveway and honked his horn. Patti Cake ran to the car, her blouse ripped and torn from the fight that had just ensued. Chuck wanted to run into the house and fight him, but Patti Cake begged him to just drive away. When Johnny came back into the house, he was screaming and cussing. He called Chuck all kinds of names and was vowing to kill them both. He kept shouting, *"Where's my gun? I am going to teach that little bitch the lesson of her life! Where's my god damned gun?!"* Gail was berserk, crying and yelling at Johnny to stop. Brave little Dottie Bug must have had an angel with her that night. She was scared to death, but when she heard what the wicked stepfather was looking for, as if someone was telling her what to do, she ran to her mama's room, found the gun Johnny hid under the bed, pulled the firing pin out of the rifle and slid it back under the bed. By the time Johnny found the gun and ran out of the house cussing, Dottie Bug was safe back in her room, again scared and not knowing what was going on.

Chuck had taken Patti Cake to his mothers house for the night to keep her safe. She had managed to escape him this time, but it wasn't over. Very shortly after this happened, Patti Cake told her mother that she and Chuck were going to run away and get married. Gail was not upset at all. Instead, she seemed almost relieved that Patti Cake was getting out of the house. When Gail brought it up to Johnny, he said it was fine with him. He was just glad that his biggest problem was leaving. They were married on April 2, 1960 in Ringgold, Georgia. Patti Cake was not quite 15 years old and still had three years of school left before graduating and Chuck had only just graduated from high school.

They visited her mother and her sisters as often as they could, but only when Johnny was at work. That November, Gail invited them to have Thanksgiving dinner at her house. You could feel the tension in the air and everyone was thankful that nothing happened to cause a stir. After dinner, Patti Cake invited her sister Dottie Bug to spend the night at her and Chuck's house. They were going to drive downtown to watch the lighting of Rich's Great Christmas Tree and she would really enjoy seeing the sight and listening to the music. Dottie Bug lit up like a Christmas tree with excitement and Gail was happy for her to go.

Johnny had a different idea. He said *"No"*. Patti Cake started arguing with him about taking Dottie Bug and he lunged forward at her as if to hit her. Just as fast as he lunged forward, Chuck jumped in between them, grabbing Johnny's arm. They began to wrestle and fight each other. They ended up outside on the front porch, falling down the steps that led to the ground. The three ladies were standing above them screaming and begging them to stop fighting. Chuck pinned Johnny to the ground and reached around into his pocket. He pulled a pocket knife out, opened it up and stuck it right up to Johnny's throat. *"You son-of-*

a-bitch! You are never going to hurt her again!" Just in the knick of time, Gail's father Ernest drove up into the driveway. He jumped out, ran over to the fight yelling, *"Stop it! Stop it right now!"* Pappy Lloyd had saved Johnny's life that night.

Chapter Twelve

Life Continues for Dottie Bug

WITH PATTI CAKE MARRIED and off living with Chuck, Dottie Bug had a huge void in her life. She no longer had the comfort of her big sister. She missed the only person in her life that listened to her dreams. They had shared so much love for each other and bared so much pain together. Now she felt as though she was alone to face the problems of life with her mother, her little sister, and "Him". She knew why Patti Cake left, but it wasn't any easier for her.

As time passed, Dottie Bug matured into a young woman and began to fill out in the places young women do. Johnny used to tease Dottie Bug about her breasts, calling them "little green apples". He used to laugh and tell her *"You're mamas gonna have to buy you a bra soon!"* Then he would look at her in the way he looked at her mama. It would make Dottie Bug so nervous that she became self-conscious about her breasts. She began to slump her shoulders in order that her "little green apples" were not so noticeable. Now, 40 years later, she still fights poor posture.

Life did not change much for Gail and Johnny. She still catered to his every need but he started to drink and cursed even more. With Patti Cake gone, his attentions turned more towards Dottie Bug than before. Just like her sister, she found out that she could not have friends over to the house. In fact, she didn't have many friends at all because she was too embarrassed to bring anyone home. Every time she tried, Johnny would be drunk and rude. He would curse, belch, and fart loudly, then laugh about it.

Dottie Bug had learned from her sister that back talking him only made him worse. She tried her best to avoid conflicts with him. He would utilize any opportunity he found as an excuse to touch her. He would pick fights with her just so he had an excuse to beat her with his belt. While he was swinging the belt, he was fondling her, touching her in places that were so very inappropriate. *"Where is my mama when all this is happening?"* she kept asking herself. He made her sick at her stomach just to look at him. She understood well how Patti Cake felt and she wanted out as well. She hated not having friends, she hated the way he beat her and she hated the way he made her feel dirty with his looks. She hated him for making her give her toys to her little sister when she cried. She hated her mother for letting all this happen. She was filled with hate for life itself.

As if her life so far was not traumatizing enough, during the summer before she started 8th grade, events unfolded that would scar her emotionally forever. Her mama and stepfather were arguing again. It was about 11:30 in the evening. She had not been in bed long, and they were fighting tremendously, only it was different. His voice was low and pleading. His words slurred so badly she could hardly understand what he was saying but he kept repeating it over and over. He was begging for forgiveness. *"I can't help myself! I am in love with Dottie Bug!"* She was numb with disbelief. He kept telling Gail over again how sorry he was, but he still kept telling her how much he was in love with her daughter. Dottie Bug wanted to die that night. She was instantly so afraid of him. What would happen if he tried to show it? Would he try to rape her? Surely, her mother would do something. Her mama wouldn't let a grown man do anything wrong to a helpless child. What did Gail do? Nothing. Oh, she cried a lot, but it was because he had broken her heart, not because of his desire for her daughter.

After all she had done for him, she was crushed that he had professed his love for her daughter instead of her. The only defense she offered for her daughter was an almost childish threat for him to stay from her little girl. Dottie Bug was so sure that Gail would pack up their bags the next day and leave this sick man and his perverted mind. How could she not? How could she live with him, knowing what his thoughts were?

The next day, Dottie Bug woke up in her room as if nothing happened the night before. Gail had not packed anything. Gail never spoke of the previous nights events. Never mentioned what was discussed. That is the very minute Dottie Bug lost respect for her mother and She looked around in her room and realized how alone she was. Alone to face everything that happened. She never mentioned anything to anyone about the night before. She was so close to giving up. Her life had been such a nightmare with out her best friend to comfort her. Her thoughts turned to suicide. She even tried by cutting one of her wrists, but all she managed to do was cause a scar. That scar remains on her wrist even today to constantly remind her just how miserable she had become.

She simply kept the whole nightmare to herself, her mind conjuring up scenarios of people accusing her of tempting him, luring him on, making him think it was ok to want her the way he did. She did not feel she could convince anyone their thoughts were far from the truth, nor did she think anyone would believe that he could have said the things he said. Therefore, she kept quiet, and she prayed. She prayed that God would show her a way out.

As soon as Dottie Bug started High School, she started dating boys. She had been dating for three years when one of the boys asked her to marry him. He was 18 years old. She was sixteen years old and too young to marry without permission, but just like Patti Cake, Gail gladly signed her daughter out of the house. Sure, why not! She had long felt that Patti Cake and Dottie Bug were excess baggage, and she felt that her two daughters came between her and happiness with Johnny and little Jenny. Now, she could get back to the perfect life she had wanted so badly.

On September 3, 1964, Maria Diane Sanders married Robert Monroe. Shortly after the end of her 10th grade of high school she left behind the drinking, the cursing, her little sister, and even her mother. She wanted so badly to disappear and make a new, happy life with her own handsome man. She was so sure that God had finally delivered her from the hell she had always known!

Chapter Thirteen

Sisters Rejoin and Families Complete

WITH PATTI CAKE AND DOTTIE BUG married and out of the house, the two lovers had the time of their lives, enjoying each other with no other cares in the world. Little Sister Jenny was "pawned off" on Patti Cake or Dottie Bug on a regular basis, and, just like her two older sisters, Jenny left her mama and daddy as soon as she could, leaving home at 15 years old to start her own legacy, or just run from the one she knew. Now Johnny and Gail were alone and their dreams had finally come true.

Panama City Beach was their new hot spot, and they traveled there almost every weekend. Johnny had been with Delta Airlines long enough to have several weeks of vacation and other personal time. He would borrow money from the credit union, or take cash off their MasterCard and they would hit the road. They would disappear for days or weeks and laugh because no one knew where they were going or when they would be back.

In the early 1970's, Johnny's youngest brother died in the Vietnam War. His parents took the insurance money they received and bought 5 acres of untouched land on an old beautiful lake. They divided the land and deeded three of those acres to Johnny and Gail. Now Johnny and Gail could have sex whenever they wanted, wherever they wanted. They could smoke, drink, and fish all the time. That is just what they did. Sure, Johnny worked hard to clear the land and make beautiful gardens for them, but the result was always the same. He and Gail were together.

Meanwhile, Patti Cake and Dottie Bug were married, having children of their own, and trying not to think about the way things were when they were young. They tried to forget it all by devoting themselves to the children they loved so much. They spent as much time together as they could. Patti Cake's husband Chuck, and Dottie Bug's husband Robert - she called him "Bobby" - started working at Eastern Airlines at the same time. Life with the Sanders girls filled with times spent trying to make up for lost years.

Patti Cake and Chuck had two boys and two girls. Dottie Bug and Bobby had three boys. Their husbands became best friends, and their children played together, sleeping over with each other on the weekend, or going camping. Patti Cake and Dottie Bug gave wonderful birthday parties for their kids. Holidays were an extra special occasion, with the wonderful decorations Patti

Cake would put together and the beautiful cakes Dottie Bug would make. The two women loved each other's kids as much as they loved their own and they both vowed that their children would have everything they did not. They also decided their children would not know the humiliation they felt when they were growing up.

Patti Cake began a career in retail and Dottie Bug was hard at work with the government. They were both determined to survive in their chosen paths. Patti Cake did not want to continue working for the $3.00 or so per hour her education level provided for, so she decided to go back to finish her education. With her oldest daughter in school, a newborn in her arms and a two year old in tow, she went to Metropolitan College on Stewart Avenue in Atlanta, studied hard for months and finally obtained her GED. Even with three children, she managed to proudly graduate high in her class.

Dottie Bug had married two years before she graduated high school. She also found it necessary to finish her education, so she obtained her GED through one of the local high schools shortly after she was married. After her third child was born, she enrolled in Clayton State College where she completed several courses that would aid in the development of her career.

By now, Johnny and Gail were aging, and it was taking a toll on their sex life. Johnny had developed diabetes from alcohol abuse. One of the side effects is impotency, so his manhood had been challenged, leaving both of them frustrated. Even that didn't stop them from being alone and away from the world as much as possible. They still traveled to Panama City often, and they had begun visiting their daughter Jenny regularly. Jenny and her family now lived in Mobile, Alabama. Their trip to Mobile was a different excuse to go fishing, and soon they were going to Dolphin Island on a regular basis.

When their children were young, Patti Cake and Dottie Bug never mentioned how their grandparents had acted years earlier. As the years passed, and as the two of them began to mellow, Gail and Johnny started including the families on their trips to Florida, delighting everyone. To their children, Gail was Granny and Johnny was Papa. Patti Cake and Dottie Bug's children loved to visit their Granny and Papa. Most Sunday's, both families would gather to go to "Granny and Papa's" house for dinner.

Yes, Gail began to evolve into a loving mother and grandmother. She would love to cook for them and always cooked a feast. Everyone loved her food. The three acres of land developed into very rich farmland and they would raise enough to feed a literal army. At one time, they had two large capacity freezers brimming with frozen vegetables. The cabinets and even the closets were packed with beautiful canned tomatoes, green beans, pickles, and the best jellies anyone had ever tasted. She fed neighbors, friends, friends of friends, but mostly, she made sure that her family left with boxes and bags full of food. One of her favorite anecdotes was *"Rithmatik sez divide!"* Then she would pile high a "to-go" box for whoever was there.

Gail would light up like a candle when people drove up. Johnny, on the other hand, still had his moods. When company came, he would sit in front of the television and visitors were lucky to even get a hand wave as they walked in. That was just the way life was on Green Valley Drive in Fairburn, Georgia.

Patti Cake and Dottie Bug slowly began talking about their life at 104 South Lee Street. They both had basically the same memories, each with their own perspective. However, some conflicting stories and explanations started emerging regarding their real daddy and their older sister. Gail had explained to each of her two daughter's that her Granny Sanders had killed their older sister when she was a baby, but they both had a slightly different story. How could it be? Had it been so long that their mama had forgotten or become confused? They started asking their mama what really happened. Gail would simply tell them, *"You'll find out sooner or later."* She would just change the subject, leaving the girls with no answer.

Each time they saw her, the girls - now grown women - they would prod their mother for details. They finally got a different story from her. This story made more sense to them and they accepted it as a plausible alternative to the original tale. Gail, herself, had a hard time remembering what story she had told each of them, so she was relieved when she could tell them both the same story. A fresh start on an old lie, so to speak.

They were sitting at the dinner table on Green Valley Drive, Gail's two daughters listening intently. Gail went on to apologize for not telling them long ago, but she did not think they would like the real truth. She said their daddy had been in a fight during a card game. He was caught cheating by the wife of one of the other players. She explained that a fight ensued and one of them beat him in the head with a frying pan, causing him to die a day or two later.

So, Gail had come up with a *half-truth*. She was proud of that story. It was true enough to remember and was even intriguing enough to begin telling to everyone. Soon, even the grandchildren were being told the story. It wasn't long before everyone knew it, and it had become fact. She even got bold enough to add in a few names of some of the people there.

She explained that Her brother-in-law, Ted Manns, his brother Jeff Manns, and a friend of theirs named Davey James were all playing poker. A fight broke out, all three were arrested, and Davey James was the one they convicted for his murder. There were more questions about some of the story, but it was mostly *"who was he related to?"* or *"what happened to him?" "did you still speak at family functions?"* and the like. Years passed and the questions finally died. Gail was happy to have a credible story. After all, she didn't have to remember her lie, because everyone else remembered it for her.

Patti Cake and Dottie Bugs families got older, and their lives became filled with events that kept them from spending time together as they once had. Soon, the only tie they could manage to hold onto was Granny and Papa's house. They still enjoyed going, and would spend hours there, talking as though no time had passed. It all seemed good, and anyone would have thought Granny and Papa would be proud to have all of them. Yet, even though they had three daughters, it seemed as though one of them stood out more than the other two. There were eleven grandchildren total. Even though Gail and Johnny claimed to really love them all, the ones they would talk about the most were Jenny's children.

Jenny bore only four of their grandchildren, and Jenny and her family were never around. Yet, despite the distance between her and her older sisters, you would think she had the only grandchildren Gail and Johnny had, especially the youngest girl. Granted, she was a beautiful baby. She had the most beautiful ringlets of hair, identical to Shirley Temple's. But everyone would get tired of hearing about her over and over. Gail and Johnny were so charmed by their movie star look-a-like that they built a mini-shrine in her honor. For years, all the grand children had pictures on the walls, but only one of them had an entire entertainment center devoted just to them. It became a joke amongst the other children and grandchildren.

Chapter Fourteen

The Sick Years

AS TIME PASSED AND THE VISITS to see Gail and Johnny lessened in length and lessened in frequency Gail found her self missing out on life once again. Johnny was no longer able to satisfy her sexually, and he seldom wanted to go fishing. His diabetes had taken over his body and his health was failing. He was no longer enough for her. She yearned for her children. She was so happy to see anyone that came to visit that she would immediately do what came naturally to her. She cooked. Then she would eat with everyone that showed up. She enjoyed watching them enjoying themselves with her food. It was her chance to visit with everyone and in her mind she felt worthy and wanted. She wanted more, though.

It is true that you should be careful what you wish for, because you find out the grass is not always greener. After all the years of trying to be away from everybody, the two had finally gotten what they wanted and she quickly grew tired of being there alone so much. Gail reached out for the one thing that made her happy - food. She kept gaining weight. Along with that weight, she began having heart problems. Heart problems led to lung problems. Soon she was taking multiple prescriptions and the doctors visits became very regular. Johnny became jealous of the times she spent with her own doctors, so Gail soon started going to Johnny's doctor. This way, Johnny could sit in on the visits without worrying about what was going on in the other room.

In later years, all the children and grandchildren could not help but feel they used the same doctor because Johnny was afraid Gail would be ill with something that he didn't have, or that he would come down with something she didn't have. This competition later resulted in alternate visits to the doctor and even the hospital. Sometimes they would spend weeks back and forth to Clayton General Hospital, now Southern Regional Hospital. Periodically, they would be in the hospital at the same time, on different floors. It was almost comical.

Gail started calling Patti Cake and Dottie Bug and asking them to come and visit. They would both go almost every time she asked, but times arose when they were too busy, or they had other things they had to do. It was the times when they told their mother they couldn't that she devised a plan to guilt them into coming down. She would call them and tell them how sick she felt. This worked to get them down there until they figured out that little ploy. Her next efforts were to call them crying. Blubbering on the phone that no one loved her and she sure wished someone would come down. That also worked for a while. Soon Gail found her phone calls going to busy signals, which would last for hours. When busy signals changed to answering machines, her messages became cries for help. She would leave messages urgent in nature, like *"Please call me, I have something really important to tell you."* When guilt would drive them to call her "just in case" she would giggle and say, *"I just wanted to tell you I love you".*

These kinds of games continued for years. Dottie Bug was very active in her job with the government and since she and Bobby had divorced several years ago, she was also working very hard to raise three boys on her own. Life was challenging enough without her mother putting the extra stress of guilt on her. Patti Cake, a successful Sales Manager, had her own set of concerns with her family. But, each time, the two grown women would alter their busy lives because they loved their mother and they felt guilty. *"What if this is real?"* they kept asking themselves.

As she got older and she couldn't get around as much as she used to, she used to call her daughters and ask them to bring her something to eat. Even with two freezers full of food wasting away, and still so much food in her cabinets, she had developed a taste for Kentucky Fried Chicken. She craved Kentucky Fried Chicken and a biscuit. When Johnny started buying her Burger King Hamburgers, she thought she was in heaven. She ate it whenever she could. Soon, even the grandchildren who came to visit her knew she loved chicken and hamburgers. They brought her food every time they came to visit, and she would eat with whoever came down. Sometimes, she would eat four and five times a day. Her famous words were, *"I'll just have a little bite with you."* This went on for about 15 years. Patti Cake and Dottie Bug had pretty much forgotten about the physical abuse they received when they were young. Looking back, it was not as bad as the abuse they would be subjected to over the next period of their lives.

It took him years, but Johnny's health was getting worse and he was finally mellowing out and started to enjoy the family he had neglected so much. He still had his quirks, but the constant family interactions changed him- a little. He got so very sick one night that he ended up throwing up part of the lining in his stomach, which caused a chain reaction of illnesses from infections. Gail had to change the way she cooked for him, changing to bland diets that consisted of no salts, low carbohydrates, and absolutely no sugars. He kept saying he was going to live forever and he fought the diet changes.

He started reading books about Tao, he took vitamins, tried herbal substitutes, but he eventually landed back into the bad eating habits that had put him I the condition he was in. On his birthday one year, his body's present to himself was a heart attack that left him largely under her control. Already weak from her own health problems, caring for him like she did landed her in the hospital a short time later. She, too, had a heart attack. (Do you see a pattern developing?) When she came home, the real race to be first with a new illness started. Even though he was recuperating from his heart attack, she felt that he should dote on her the way she doted on him. They were taking so much medication at this point that most of their day was consumed with which pill they should take when.

Whatever symptom one had, the other got. When one of them got a kidney infection, the other would follow suit. Sometimes the doctors would find a reason for the illness, but more often, the doctor would just pacify them by writing them a prescription for what ever they wanted. Everyone thought that the doctor was just a quack that had found a gold mine of insurance claims. The pharmacy loved the steady hundreds of dollars each month coming in from these two people who exaggerated illnesses to the point of ridicule from their family.

All the years of Lucky Strikes and Camel filter-less cigarettes took a toll on her and Gail was legitimately diagnosed with emphysema, which caused major bouts of asthma and lung congestion. Maybe it was the medications, or maybe it was the illnesses, but Johnny and Gail both felt everyone should cater to them. Each would blame the other for their illnesses, neither of them accepting their fate as their own fault.

Gail was in her 50's when she started loosing a grip on reality. The lake front property where they had lived for so many years was pure country. There was nothing in the immediate area but six homes, a lake, and a dirt road that was so narrow two cars could not go by each other without pulling off into the grass. The most common visit from anything God created was a stray dog or cat, or maybe a rabbit or deer that may be wandering around. The back of the house was nothing but trees. Nothing but trees and more trees stood behind a six feet high fence. Whatever she and Johnny had been involved in when they were younger, for some reason, she started to suspect that the FBI was watching her. She would run to the front window over looking the lake and swear she saw someone looking in. They lived the rest of their lives with closed curtains and blinds shut. The house became dark and musty smelling.

They had guns - one rifle in the bedroom and one 410 shotgun in the closet behind the front door. Gail used to amuse her family by telling them she was going to get her gun and *"410 their ass!"* To the grandchildren, she was just being Granny, but to the adults, she really was becoming something to worry about.

She had names for all the animals. Not uncommon, you think? Maybe not, unless you start carrying on conversations with them and getting the news of the neighborhood from them. Now, *that's odd!* (Although years later, when she would tell you *"a little bird told me"*, you would almost believe her.)

With her asthma came her intolerance to the smell of food cooking. She said it made her *"choke to death"*. She still wanted to eat, however, so, Johnny started doing some of the cooking on the front porch with an electric skillet. He made her bacon for breakfast everyday.

Johnny had taken early retirement. Actually, it was a medical retirement. He decided it would be better to take an early medical retirement than risk being fired after all those years of service. He needed the benefits Delta offered him because both of them relied on the insurance to live. You see, besides the medical conditions that caused him to miss work, she had started doing to him what she had done to her daughters. She would call his job and tell them that he needed to come home right away because she was having one of her attacks. He would leave Delta and drive home quick as possible to find that she was just lonely, or that she was not sick at all.

Dottie Bug and Patti Cake started to receive no less than one phone call every month telling them that one of the two were in the hospital. When he would call, they would ask how *she was* and he would tell them how sick *he was*. When she would call, they would ask about *Johnny* and she would exaggerate how sick *she was*. It was a constant mind game leading to unrest, bad feelings, and resentment. The same feelings they thought they had outgrown so many years ago.

When Gail would call her daughters, one of the first things she would ask for was a piece of chicken and a biscuit. Her only solace in life now was food. Pardon the expression, but she lived for it.

It had been years since they slept together sexually, and in the recent years, their sleeping habits had fluctuated so much that they rarely slept together at all. She blamed him for the lack of sex, and he was frustrated that he was no longer "a man". She ended up sleeping on the couch more often and he eventually bought her the queen size bed advertised on television that adjusted from the head and the feet. After all, she was up and down most of the night with her lung problems, why not just sleep in the living room next to the table and chairs, *right*?

Her mind continued to wander, and her ailments got more intense. She had convinced herself that most of her problems stemmed from allergies. One day she was convinced she was allergic to eggs, but the very next day she was having eggs with cheese in her biscuit. Another day she was convinced that strawberries were her only problem. No sooner had she self diagnosed that problem, she would devour Patti Cakes strawberry cake. There was nothing consistent in either of their beliefs, because they self diagnosed themselves so often and inaccurately, even they would get confused about what really ailed them. But, Gail kept eating. She was hospitalized for edema one month. When they asked her about allergies she had, Gail started naming off all sorts of drugs, foods, and smells she was allergic to, including eggs. Yet, when she was filling out her request for breakfast, what was her first choice? Eggs. The dietician came in to talk to her, thinking Gail was mistaken. Gail politely told her she could eat eggs everywhere but at home. She held firm to her loose grip on reality.

Patti Cake was at work when she received a phone call from Johnny. She knew it had to be important because Johnny had never before called her at her job. He said he had taken her mother to the hospital again. Patti Cake was so used to hearing it that it didn't really phase her anymore, but something about his voice caught her attention. He said the doctors were recommending psychiatric evaluation for her mother and he wanted her opinion. Her very words were *"Go for it! I have thought she was crazy for years!"* So, he discussed it with Gail, who immediately denied the need and would not cooperate. Johnny dropped it and it was never discussed again.

From then on, she would start crying and pouting whenever she didn't get her way. For a while, the children, the grandchildren, and even her friends would either do what she wanted, but they eventually just stopped coming around. It just wasn't the same Granny and Papa they knew and had grown up with.

Whether he just got tired, or just got tired of it, Johnny started giving in to her mood swings. He just started taking care of her and catering to her, just as she had done for him during those early years. The circle began completing quickly. He was now the browbeaten man the browbeaten woman used to be.

She had gotten too old and sick for her first love - *dancing*. She had lost the love of her life when Maxwell Jackson left her. When Payton died, she lost the second love she had known. Johnny's health ended the fourth loves, fishing and sex. Now, the only loves she had left in life, her children and grandchildren, were abandoning her. She clung so very hard to the loves she had left – a few remaining offspring's. And, of course, food.

As sick as she was, she was never too sick to eat. She ate chocolate, cheetos, hamburgers and fried chicken. As she continued to gain weight, her health got worse. Her lungs got weaker, her breathing more labored. The doctors prescribed steroids to strengthen them, but soon she had taken them so long they were more for maintenance than cure. Her arms, face and legs broke out in big blue splotches and crusty sores from steroid abuse. She no longer had the strength to walk to the bathroom to clean up, so when she could, she would take the few steps from her bed to the kitchen table where she would "bathe" herself with a wet clothe. When she had gotten so big that she couldn't raise her arms very high or bend her body very far, Johnny started cleaning her. He would wash the legs that were now turning blue and red from poor circulation.

Johnny must have still loved her deep inside, because he would do his best to get the woman he had been with for 40 odd years to his red truck and carry her to her sisters house to get her hair washed and curled. He did this until he just couldn't anymore, but by then, it was pointless to even try. Her condition was worsening by the day. Taking care of her was more than one full time job. Johnny could not do it alone anymore. He tried to get someone from the hospital to come out to visit, but his insurance had changed so that he could only get short visits once or twice per week. He tried to keep the house clean but her weak lungs "would not allow" the fresh smell of cleaning supplies.

Her mind continued to worsen as she got sicker and, soon, no one was allowed to come around with any type of cologne. She even got to the point of disallowing Johnny to use fabric sheets in the dryer. The hatred that Dottie Bug and Patti Cake felt for him so many years ago slowly turned to pity for him. The house, already dark and musty from the paranoia of thinking the FBI was watching, now smelled as a sickness smells. Johnny was beginning to wear out physically and Patti Cake and Dottie Bug would ask him how he could stand living in the environment. He would tell them *"I can't. If I had the guts, I would blow my brains out."*

Patti Cake begged her mama one day to let her clean the house and get rid of some of the germs that were breeding throughout the house. Gail told her she could clean it the day Johnny took her to the doctor. Patti Cake went to Walmart and spent $50 for cleaning supplies in addition to what she already had at her house. Patti Cake scrubbed the bathroom with Tylex and disinfected the floors. She put Limeaway in the back of the toilet to help stop some of the staining inside the toilet and she scrubbed the tub. She used almost a bottle of windex on the front windows so that sunshine could come in and you could really look out of them. She scrubbed what looked like fecal material from the floor in the dining room where her mother sat for so long. When she finished, the house looked brighter, smelled better, and felt cleaner than it had in many years. She was exhausted when she finished, but she was proud of what she had done for her mother. Later that evening, Gail called Dottie Bug and told her that Patti Cake had tried to kill her with all the perfumed cleaning supplies and that Johnny had to take the Limeaway out of the toilet because it was killing her to smell it.

On Dottie Bug's day off, she was "expected" to go to her mother's house. Patti Cake had to work later in the day, but since she wanted to see her sister, she decided to go down to her mothers before she went to work. Patti Cake had barely put her foot in the door when she saw that Dottie Bug had brought her mama a big biscuit for breakfast. She said hello to Dottie Bug and was about to speak to her mother when she was interrupted by *"UGH! You're wearing that perfume that chokes me to death! You are gonna have to leave!"* So, Patti Cake left. Hurt and bothered by her mother, but more upset at herself that she would continue to get upset by her mothers actions. Resentment built up in her, but Patti Cake was determined that she would take care of her mother regardless. She had even relocated back to the south side of town just to be there for her ailing mother and her husband.

But alas, another day off, another day devoted to running around for her mother. Gail called Patti Cake one afternoon and asked her if she would mind picking up a load of clothes that needed to be washed. She just couldn't stand smelling them wash and dry at her house. When she picked the clothes up, her mother was sitting at the dining table, just as she had for so many years. The clothes smelled pure and simply sick. She didn't want to touch them at all, but she took them home, washed them with Downy fabric softener to help the smell and when she dried them, she folded everything up so neatly, placing them in the basket. She was proud of what she had done for her mother. However, when she got back to her moms house, her mother was sitting in the same exact spot she had been in earlier and no sooner had Patti Cake opened the door to bring the clothes in, Gail yelled, *"Put them down on the floor! You used that perfume stuff! I can smell it from here! It's choking me!"* Crushed once again, she ran to her car, jumped in, locked the doors quickly and drove off in a hurry. Later that night, Dottie bug got another phone call from her mother saying that Patti Cake was trying to kill her again.

Every visit was the same. Every time Dottie Bug and Patti Cake went to visit, it wasn't by choice, it was by demand. Every time Patti Cake would leave, she would jump into her car and lock it like someone was chasing her. They both felt like they needed a bath when they left. They could smell the sickness on their clothes and on their skin. This is how they spent many months to come.

It was Christmas, 2000. Dottie Bug and Patti Cake felt obliged to visit their mother and her husband, but neither of them wanted to. Patti Cake's job in retail called for very long hours and very few days off between Thanksgiving and Christmas. She had not seen her family much this season, and she did not want to waste her time at her mothers. She and Dottie Bug decided to go down early and get it over. They both got there, gave the token Christmas gifts they had for their mother and Johnny, and spend a few "quality" minutes with them. Precious little daughter Jenny never showed up that day. Gail was looking through the packages for chocolate, not really caring what the gift was. The morning was depressing and neither of them could wait to leave. They took pictures together, just the four of them, and Dottie Bug and Patti Cake took a picture together in front of the living room fireplace. They both took pictures with their mother, neither of them realizing it would be the last pictures they had of their mother alive.

Chapter Fifteen

The Final Days

IN RECENT MONTHS, IN EVENTS that concerned every family member, Gail became certain Johnny wanted her dead. She would call around to whomever she could contact and tell them that Johnny was trying to kill her. If she had not cried wolf for so many years, maybe someone would have taken her seriously. She called Patti Cake one night crying in such pain. She said Johnny had tried to poison her. He had cooked her some fresh mushrooms and made her eat it. No one in the family has ever seen or heard of them eating mushrooms, so it took Patti Cake by surprise. She said he promised it would be good for her and she should eat them. The family nervously laughed it off, but given the circumstances, they had to consider it as possible and a flicker of doubt did rise in Patti Cakes mind.

Very often she would call Patti Cake and say, "*I have something to tell you, but I can't tell you around HIM.*" Every time Patti Cake would see her and ask what it was she wanted to say, she would say, "*Not now, it's not the right time.*" She would call Patti Cake's oldest son and tell him the same thing. Her reaction to him would be the same. Only now, looking back, can we speculate what it was she wanted so badly to say.

Her condition had worsened so greatly that Johnny moved her potty from beside the bed over to the kitchen table so that when she had the urge to go, she would not have to struggle too much. She spent the last few months of her life sleeping on the hospital bed at night, then alternating between a portable potty and a dining chair. One could not help but feel sorry seeing this once vibrant young woman, full of life reduced to the humiliation of a portable potty sitting a few feet away from her. He kept a rag on the table for her to use to clean herself when needed.

It was towards the end of January 2001 and Patti Cake was finally able to take a day of comp time from the long holiday season. She had set some goals for 2001. Since she had been on such a roller coaster ride with her mother and Johnny, number one on her list was taking better care of herself and worrying less about her mother and Johnny. She had just started painting her shutters when the phone rang. In her mind she thought, *"Ok, lets see. My only day off in a long time, who could it be?"* She already knew it was her mother calling and she started not to answer. She picked up the phone and when she said hello, she heard Johnny on the other end saying *"Patti Cake, I need your help. Your mother has fallen and I think she has broken her leg and I can't pick her up."* Patti Cakes first reaction was, *"You've got to be kidding me, right? I just started painting my shutters and I've got on my old painting clothes!"* The way he said it, she was sure he made it up. *"Don't worry about it, then. I will get someone else to help!"* Pissed off at her self, Patti Cake said, *"No, you don't have to do that. I'll be right there."* She changed her clothes, and cursing the whole way there, drove up in her mother's yard, surprised that the medics were there. Johnny had apparently hung up the phone with Patti Cake and called 911 for help.

It took three men to pick her up, put her on the stretcher and carry her to the van waiting outside. They took her to Southern Regional Hospital where they found she had broken her leg at the knee and cracked her arm from the elbow to the wrist when she fell. She spent three agonizing weeks in the hospital. Her body was bruised from falling. As Patti Cake thought about her mother's accusation of Johnny of trying to kill her, the thought did creep up that perhaps Johnny had something to do with it. But, apparently she was trying to get from the bed to the table and her legs were too weak to hold up her huge body.

Gail did not respond to the treatments she was receiving for her arm and leg. It took several days before the swelling in her arm would go down enough for them to even put a cast on it and her leg was so swollen all they could do was wrap it in a brace, hoping the swelling would go down. She refused to work with the therapist. Instead, she would end up screaming with pain. She refused to eat what they wanted her to eat and finally they told Johnny that there was truly nothing else they could do for her and recommended he place her in a convalescent nursing home. He found a very nice place not far from where Patti Cake lived; he arranged everything for her, and called the family to let them know where she would be.

When the ambulance arrived that day, Dottie Bug, Patti Cake, and Patti Cake's daughter, Lanie were waiting on her. The two girls could not believe how frail and old she looked right then. The hospital had given her a shot to calm her enough to travel in the ambulance so she was almost unconscious. The nurses met the drivers at the door and escorted them to her room. Gail mumbled something to her daughters as they wheeled her into her new home, but no one could understand exactly what she was saying. After a short while, the nurses allowed the girls into their mama's room. She had a semi-private room that looked much like her hospital room at Southern Regional Hospital. The only real differences were the landscaping outside and the type of bed. This bed had bars over the head that she was going to need when she started her physical therapy or when she wanted to move around in the bed.

Patti Cake and Dottie Bug were sitting there when she became coherent enough to speak. Patti Cake asked her if she liked her new room. Gail responded in a low, groggy, sad little voice, *"I don't even know where I am."*

For the next three weeks, Patti Cake visited her a few times each week, but her daughter Lanie was there almost everyday standing vigil to make sure her Granny was taken care of. Dottie Bug lived two hours away from there, and she was working hard to finalize her job duties so she could retire from the government. As bad as she wanted, it wasn't physically possible for her to spend the time traveling the highways. Johnny's eyesight had gotten so bad that he could not drive at night, so he would come in as soon as the day light made it visible enough, then leave before he lost his depth perception.

The nurses told her she could not wear the hospital gown anymore, so Patti Cake went to Walmart and bought three simple, but comfortable housecoats for her mama to wear. Gail loved the blue one most of all and wanted to wear it all the time. She said the other two didn't fit her right, even though Patti Cake knew they were all the same size.

Gail wouldn't even try to get better. She resisted all attempts to get better and soon the once patient nursing staff started to get irritated. Gail lie in her bed all-day, moaning and complaining that she was dying. Even the old lady that was sharing the room with her showed signs of irritation. She was brought there because she had a nerve problem that left her without speech and only partial mobility. But just because she could not speak did not mean she could not hear. One afternoon the nurses brought the two ladies food in and sat it between the beds for them to eat. Gail was moaning and groaning about how she was dieing inside and her roommate used all her strength to push the tray of food over towards Gail, as if to say, *"SHUT UP!"* They could not help but laugh at the display of anger from this sweet little woman. After all, their mother did have a way of making anyone want to scream, and this lady had simply had enough. From then on, the old woman's daughter came in each day and took her mother to the recreation room for lunch and dinner. That is where she ate the rest of the time Gail was a resident.

After the first week, the nurses decided that Gail was not going to try to use the bars over her bed, so they just removed them. She wasn't getting any better and constantly complained that she was sick at her stomach. She wouldn't eat anymore and cried hard because her stomach hurt her so bad. She had started swelling again, and the doctors found a blot clot behind the fractured knee. Her fingers were turning purple and the sores she got from the steroid abuse were beginning to ooze puss faster than the bandages could be changed.

By the third week, Johnny was all but exhausted. His health was failing because of the stresses he faced. Not only did he have his wife to worry about, he still had to think about his medications and his diet. He also worried so much about the three acres of responsibility that had been neglected for so long. He was turning a grayish color that worried all the kids, but he kept going. Toward the end of the third week, Gail actually seemed in better spirits. She told everyone that she couldn't wait to get better so she could come home and visit with everyone. Dottie Bug and even precious little Jenny came to visit her. Since she seemed to be doing better, Patti Cake decided to take one of the days of vacation she had and do some of the things around her house that she had been neglecting. When she talked to Johnny earlier that morning, he asked if she would be there and she told him she wasn't sure because she really had some things to take care of.

Around 5:00 that afternoon, Patti Cake talked to Dottie Bug. Johnny had called Dottie Bug and asked if she had any money he could borrow. They both knew how embarrassed he had to be to ask for it, but he wanted to buy Gail a coke the next day and he had no money to do it. After all these years, and after all he was going through with her, Johnny still loved Gail so very much. He wanted to do something nice for her just to try and cheer her up. Patti Cake immediately hung up the phone and called her mama's room. Johnny answered the phone and *"Daddy, don't go anywhere. I will be down there in a minute."*

Patti Cake was in her car and there in less than 15 minutes. When she drove up, he was standing at his truck with a sad look on his face. She asked how her mama was doing. He said, *"I don't know Patti Cake, I don't think she is going to get any better." "I don't think so either, daddy."* We walked into the building toward her room. He staggered at one point and fell against the wall. *"Are you ok?" "Yeah, I'm just tired."* They walked into her room and she was lying with a cloth on her head. I touched her broken leg and said *"Mama, I've come to see you."* With her good hand, Gail pulled the cloth off her forehead and so sweetly said, *"Patti Cake, I am so sick." "I know, Mama. I know."* Patti Cake went to the side of the bed her mama was lying in and put her purse down. She sat by the window but Johnny stayed standing. *"Mama, I am going to get something to eat. You visit with Patti Cake for a minute."* As he turned to walk away, Patti Cake called for him to wait for a second. She reached into her purse to get the reason she came today- the $25 she had folded up before she left her house. She walked over to him and placed it in his hand. He turned and walked toward the door, stopping for a second to see what it was. Big tears came in his eyes as he turned and softly said, *"Thank you."* She smiled at him and whispered, *"Your welcome."*

Patti Cake had accomplished what she came for and her initial impulse was to leave behind him. Instead, she decided to sit there next to her mother, looking at the woman who had broken her heart. She got a really long look at the reason she had existed for the past few years, and as she looked at this old, sick woman, she realized just how much she loved her mother. How many times had she resented the way her mother manipulated her? How many times had she wondered how long she could keep going on living the way she had been living? All those feelings of pure resentment left her body that night. All she could think about was how she wished her mother could get better. She asked her mother if she would like to have her hair combed.

Gail smiled at her oldest daughter and said so innocently, *"Oh, yea. It hasn't been combed in so long."* As Patti Cake combed her hair back from her face, her mama said in almost a whisper, *"Patti Cake, you know what I really need?" "What, mama?" "Will you clean my teeth for me? They feel so nasty. They haven't been cleaned since I got here."* Patti Cake cringed inside just thinking about it, but she took her mothers false teeth out of her mouth and had them soaking before she knew it. How could she say no right now? While they were soaking, Patti Cake rubbed her mama's arms and legs with the cream that was on the nightstand. She could tell that all this pampering was making her mother more relaxed and comfortable. *"Oh, this feels so good, Patti Cake. Thank you so much."* Patti Cake finished by washing her mothers face and applying the cream as she had the arms and legs. All the while being thanked over and over again for doing it.

Patti Cake sat next to her, holding her hand and watching. Then she realized that she didn't see the Reese's peanut butter cup she bought her last time she was there. *"Mama, did you eat all your chocolate?" "No, someone put it in the drawer over there and I can't reach it. I haven't had the first bite."* Patti Cake opened the drawer, reached in and took out one of the peanut butter cups. She placed it in her mother's mouth and her mother got a great big grin on her face. *"Oh, this is so, so good!" "You want another piece, mama?" "No, just save them for me for later."*

Patti Cake sat for the longest time in the room with her mother, just sitting and watching. Her mother wasn't crying and complaining as she had been. Perhaps it was because she felt better just having been cleaned up some. It was getting late and Patti Cake had to be leaving, but she wanted to take advantage of this moment to ask her mother one more question. *"Mother, you have been telling me for so long that you have something you want to tell me. What are you trying to tell me?"* Gail closed her eyes and said very softly, *"Not now, Patti Cake."* Patti Cake kissed her good night, told her how much she loved her, and drove home with the most peaceful feeling she had felt in forever. Patti Cake had no clue it was the last time she would see her mother in that home. The very next day, Johnny called Patti Cake and she knew from the tone of his voice there was something wrong. *"They've taken your mama to Fayette Community Hospital. She has blood in her bowels and they don't know where it is coming from."* *"I'll be right there!"*

While Patti Cake was hurriedly putting her clothes on to go to the hospital, she couldn't help but feel grateful for the night before with her mother. She was also thankful that they were sending her to Fayette Community Hospital instead of the hospital where their quack doctors worked. She had tried to get them to change for years, but they were both stubborn. Finally, she knew her mother was going to be in good hands. She drove up just as they were getting her out of the ambulance. She met her stepfather as they were going in. God, how he looked like he should be the patient! She took him inside and they went to admissions to fill out whatever paperwork needed to be done and Johnny went back to be with Gail. Patti Cake immediately called Dottie Bug and told her the situation. Dottie Bug was almost two hours away but she would hurry to get there.

After a while, he came out and asked if she would like to go back for a minute. When Patti Cake went back to the little room, she found her mother lying there with a sheet to keep her from getting too cold. Gail was lying there and acting so strong, her daughter couldn't help but be proud of her. She thought back to the night before and thought how funny things can be. She had such a wonderful night with her mother and was so very grateful. When the door opened, a man walked in and introduced himself as Dr. Almond. Patti Cake liked him immediately and joked with him about all the doctors looking so young these days. He said he was 38, but most days didn't feel as young as he seemed. He told Gail that he was going to examine her. He was going to be gentle with her but it may hurt a little. Patti Cake walked away for a minute to give her some privacy during the exam, ever so proud of her mother for being so strong right now. When the doctor put the sheet back over her mother, Patti Cake walked back to the bed. The doctor looked Patti Cake in the eyes and for a second she saw much pain in his face.

"Mrs. Wyatt, you are a very sick woman. You know that, don't you?" He spoke very softly to her, asking her questions about her hernia and how long she had it. He asked if she had ever had a test to check for blockages in her intestines. Patti Cake knew some of the answers her mother was giving were wrong, but she let her talk. The doctor told Gail they would do everything they could to make her more comfortable, but they needed to ask one question. *"If anything goes wrong, do you want us to hook you up to life support?"* With all the strength Gail could muster, she grabbed him by the hand and said, *"Don't let me die!"* Patti Cake tried to explain that life support is what they use to keep you alive. The doctor explained to Gail that if she goes on life support, once the brain ceases to function, the rest of the body will slowly shut down as well. Gail looked like a scared little girl by this point. Patti Cake stopped the doctor by laying her hand on his arm and asked her to wait while she went to get her stepfather. Patti Cake stepped out of the room and found him in a chair, slumped over like an old man. *"Daddy, you need to come in here. The doctor is talking to mama about life support."* Johnny didn't say a word, he just stood up and

walked into the room with his wife and the doctor that was younger than some of the grandchildren in the family.

Johnny stood next to his wife as the doctor told them all how grave the situation really was. He explained what life support would mean to the patient as well as the family. He looked down at Gail and said, *"Gail, it is your decision."* Just then, Johnny screamed out, *"DON'T LEAVE ME!"* Before Patti Cake knew what she was doing, she had grabbed him hard on the back of his arm and pinched him with all her might. She told her mama, *"Mama, don't put the family through this! We couldn't stand to see you that way!"* Gail looked at Patti Cake and Johnny, then looked at the doctor and said, *"I don't want that."* Dr. Almond patted Gail on the hand and told her he would do everything he could to keep her with her family.

When Dottie Bug got to the hospital, Patti Cake filled her in on everything that was happening. She told her that the outlook was grim but they would do everything they could for her. Dottie Bug went in to see her mother. Patti Cake was sitting outside on a bench with her stepfather, trying to comfort him as much as she could. They had not yet determined what was causing the bleeding in her bowels, but they were looking at everything they knew to do. Dottie Bug came running through the double doors that led from the emergency room to the waiting room. She had tears in her eyes as she grabbed her sisters hand and said, *"Mama wants to be buried next to 'HIM' and 'the baby'!"* All Patti Cake could say was *"WHAT?"* They both knew who their mother was referring to. After almost 50 years of living as Mrs. John Lewis Wyatt, their mother wanted to be buried next to their real father, Walter Payton Sanders and their would-be older sister, Addy Mae Sanders. What an awkward situation their mother had placed them in once again! With all that is happening, how in the world would they handle this?

Gail was transferred to intensive care and the testing continued. The nurses tried several enemas while she was in the hospital, but her intestines were so blocked up all they accomplished was making her more uncomfortable. Once they found the problem, Dr. Almond explained in terms that Gail and the rest of the family would understand. It seems that the years of abuse Gail had given her body was such that a domino effect had finally culminated in her current condition. As her already poor diet got worse and she continued to push fatty foods into her body, her intestines continued to clog more and more. As her eating habits and lack of exercise caused constipation year after year, it had weakened her intestines. In some areas of her stomach, her intestines had hardened so much they had become almost petrified and clay-like, allowing less and less food to pass through. That is why her "belly ached" so much in recent years. Eventually, the intestines could not take the strain and hernias developed in her stomach, one of which was the size of a football.

When she fell and broke her arm and her knee, the doctors at the other hospital put her on blood thinner to avoid blood clots and after she was moved to the convalescent home, she was kept on them, but in monitored doses. The blood was coming from the area of the intestines that had been stretched thin with wear and deterioration. The sores she had were oozing because her body had no clotting ability left. The end result? A very sick woman who was considered at this point to be inoperable.

Years ago, her intestines had been the main problem, but now she was full of infections, and the infections were breeding so quickly that she would die very soon. All they could do was make her as comfortable as they could until the time came. They began giving her morphine drip to keep her comfortable. It seemed to help greatly, and she was at peace for the first time in so long. The first few days she slept most of the time. Johnny had gone home to get some rest and take his insulin. Dottie Bug had to get back to work so Patti Cake and Lanie stayed in the waiting room that Tuesday night. In the wee hours on Wednesday, the nurse came in and said, *"Your mama is awake, would you like to come and visit?"* To Patti Cakes surprise, she found her mother in good spirits! The nurses said they would be giving her blood soon so they couldn't stay back there long.

They kissed her on the forehead and she told them she loved them. She said she wasn't in pain anymore but she was hungry and they wouldn't give her anything to eat. *"They will soon, Mama, I promise."* Patti Cake assured her mother, knowing it was not likely to happen. A few hours later Patti Cake walked back into the room to visit a minute. She was startled to hear her mama talking to someone. *"Mama? What are you saying?"* *"Move!"* she told her daughter, *"I am not talking to you, I am talking to him."* She was actually carrying on a conversation with Payton, her first husband and the girl's real daddy. Was it the morphine talking or was he actually in the room with her? Patti Cake wasn't sure.

She and her sister Dottie Bug had to hurry and make some decisions. First, they had to tell Johnny what their mother had decided. Then, they had to find out who to talk to about the grave sites. It had been years since either of them had talked to anyone who might know about the burial plots. Patti Cake knew exactly where the sites were, and even though there was only a bread pan marking the two graves, she knew exactly how to find them. So, in between trips to the hospital over the next days, Dottie Bug and Patti Cake would make trips to courthouses and other venues to find what they would need to honor their mother's last wishes. What they unfolded was not only answers to some questions, but questions to some questions they had never fathomed to ask. The final pages of this book are filled with more intrigue and more information than either of them had ever read in a book or seen on a movie. Through it all, what they found out brought them closer to their mother than they had ever been before and has since sparked curiosities that may never be answered.

Gail moved in and out of consciousness each day. Each time she was alert, she would carry on with the nurses or the children, all of them laughing because she was so funny to be around. She was her old self again joking and making everyone remember just how she used to be. She was "Granny" once again. Isn't it so odd how pain can change a person, and how no pain can bring them right back?

Even though Gail had decided she did not want any life support, on two occasions over the next week, the nurses brought her back to life and kept her going. Yes, they went against the wishes of the patient, but the nurses at Fayette Community Hospital wanted to make sure they did everything that was medically possible. In the end, the family would be eternally grateful to them - even though the last few days of her life was spent on life support. What happened over the next few days was so spiritual and precious that neither Patti Cake nor Dottie Bug would write it down.

To each of them, those visits with their mother in the last few days before she went to her eternal home relieved them of years of anger, resentment, and bitterness for anything she might have lacked when she was alive. God was truly in the room with her and no one will ever be able to dispute it. He was in the room with her family. There were angels walking the hallways of Fayette Community Hospital that week. Angels that drowned the bad, and accentuated the good, holding their newest companion on earth long enough to allow those that loved her to join, reminisce, and rejoice the woman known as "Granny".

In the beginning of this book, you were introduced to her little brother Stan. He was the youngest of the children raised by Ernest and Annie Mae Martin and he was Gail's favorite. He was the one she waited on to say goodbye. The preacher came into Gail's room. Her daughter's Dottie Bug and Patti Cake, Patti Cake's daughter Lanie, and Gail's brother Stan and his wife watched and prayed with the preacher. He said a prayer for Gail and was leaning to anoint her forehead saying, *"We will leave just enough of her spirit in her body to spend some time with her family,"* when suddenly, with God as their witness, the room began to fill with an electrical energy. The over 500 pound bed, with her nearly 300 pound body laying on it, rose upward towards the ceiling as if it were rising her to Heaven. The pillows were under her leg inflated to almost twice their size. As they all stood in shock and disbelief, Gail's head and chest lifted off the bed right in front of Stan, Patti Cake, Dottie Bug and everyone else in the room. Dottie Bug turned to the nurses station to call for help, but when she turned back towards her mother, it was over. It was the most spiritual feeling that any of them had ever felt. They had just witnessed God's spirit sending His Angels to earth to carry another Angel home. Later, none of them spoke of it, for fear that no one would understand.

Patti Cake and Dottie Bug's family had already been waiting. The doctors and nurses were telling everyone that it was time. Precious Jenny had still not arrived with her family and the doctor said he was going to have to do something soon because her body was honestly imploding from the infections. Gail was floating in and out of a comatose state. When she spoke, her words were barely audible and her eyes were flickering as though she was looking around for someone. When Jenny and her bunch finally arrived, her youngest, the once movie star-look-a-like cried and didn't want to see her like that.

Gail's family gathered in the room. Even her nurse, yet another angel in the eyes of the family, stood vigil while she lay there. The doctor said it was time. He disconnected the power supply and removed the tubes from Gail's mouth and nose. Her baby brother Stan walked up to her, kissed her on the forehead, told her how much he loved her and that it was ok for her to leave. He told her not to worry and they would be fine. She took her slow breathes, each slower than the last. On February 24, 2001, at 2:11 pm, her husband, her three daughters and most of her grandchildren watched as she finally took her last breath, released it, and left this earth.

Chapter Sixteen

The Investigation

AS HER MAMA LAY THERE ON her deathbed, her health deteriorating rapidly, Dottie Bug promised her that their real daddy and their sister would get a real tombstone, even if she had to pay for it herself. Having made that commitment, she and Patti Cake had some research to do. They would need both the birth dates and death dates of both of them. They traveled to Downtown Atlanta to the Georgia Department of Vital Records. They found a birth certificate for their daddy, Walter Payton Sanders, as well as his death certificate. They were both shocked to read that the cause of death read "HOMICIDE". They were even more amazed that the place of injury was "HOME". This was news to both of them. Their daddy had been *murdered!*

Suddenly, a huge question came to their mind. *Was the secret she had been unwilling to confess to them was that she had murdered their father?* Both of them stood in awe, tears streaming down their faces. Had she tried to hide the ugly truth from them all these years? They both realized how it could have possibly driven her mad in her older years. All those times she kept saying the FBI was watching her could have been nothing more than her conscience eating at her.

Questions flooded into the minds of both the women. *"Could their mother have killed their father? Did she go to jail? Had those many months at Granny Sanders house been a time when she was taken away from them? Is this why neither of them remembered moving from Flat Shoals Road to 104 South Lee Street? Had Granny Sanders actually had custody of them while their mother was in jail?"* The death certificate stated that his mother, Martha Jean Sanders, requested an inquest. She must have suspected fowl play, otherwise why would she ask for an inquisition? They continued their search for records. Their souls burned like wildfire.

Since Patti Cake was closer to everything, they would meet at her house each morning they could and think up new questions to ask, but never veering from their task. They would go to different courthouses and search for as much information as they could find. Their mother worsened as the clocks ticked and they were running out of time. In order to honor their mother's last wishes to be buried next to him they needed proof that he had belonged to the church that owned the land. They found out his death certificate was insufficient to prove their daddy was buried at

Pleasant Grove Cemetery. They needed proof that he could have even been *allowed* to get buried there. Neither of them knowing just how soon they would need the information, just before their mama died, it was by the grace of *God himself* that they ended up with the proof that he was, in deed, buried there. By the time Gail passed away, Dottie Bug and Patti Cake had unraveled enough of the mystery to not only bury their mother in the cemetery with the rest of her deceased family, but they had also arranged for a headstone big enough for their mother, their real father, and their would-be older sister, Addy Mae. Patti Cake and Dottie Bug had finalized the funeral arrangements that Johnny was not able to handle.

Yet, their curiosity had not been satisfied. They still had questions. Now that she was gone, and that chapter of their life was closed, since they could no longer hurt her with the truth, they decided to write down the questions they had not answered. Those questions were:

        1-   *"Why was their daddy murdered?"*
        2-   *"What happened to start the fight to begin with?"*
        3-   *"Who was really involved?"*
        4-   *"Where had the fight really occurred?"*

5- *"What REALLY happened to our sister?"*
6- *"Who killed her and why?"*
7- *"Was it an accident, or intentional?"*
8- *"Was their mama questioned or locked up either time?"*
9- *"Had Patti Cake and Dottie Bug been taken from their mama because of her involvement with their daddy's death?"*
10- *"Why were they never allowed to ask questions about their Daddy or their sister?"*
11- *"Why was a gravestone never placed over either of the graves?*
12- *"Would they ever find out the truth?"*

Two weeks later, the two women on their quest for truth stood outside yet another courthouse praying,

"God, lead us to the information that we need to set our souls free. Give us some truth, God. In your name, Amen."

On the little bit of information they had- their daddy's name, and the name of Davey James – they walked into the courtroom like two detectives. They walked up to the probate court clerk and told them what they had to accomplish. The way they described the reasons they needed to know and the events that led them on their journey, the clerk was soon enthralled in their passions and was anxious, herself, to find out what really happened. They were both nervous and shaking when the clerk handed them a huge record book from that general period of time. This is what their investigations uncovered:

Their mother's brother-in-law, Ted Manns was involved. In case number 1331, he was charged with MURDER. The case was ruled "NO LAW PROCEED" and he was not sentenced for the charge.

Later, in case 1466, he was charged with five counts of ASSAULT WITH INTENT TO MURDER. He was found GUILTY and was sentenced to two years per count. He remained in prison until being paroled on March 2, 1955.

His brother, Jeff Manns, was also involved. He was found GUILTY of four counts of ASSAULT WITH THE INTENT TO MURDER. He was sentenced to ten years of prison time. He was paroled on November 17, 1955.

In case number 1330, Davey James was charged with MURDER but found NOT GUILTY. Days later, on November 28, 1951, in case number 1416, he was charged with ASSAULT WITH INTENT TO MURDER. He was found GUILTY and served five years in prison. Davey James died before he was eligible for parole.

One interesting note: In the murder case of Walter Payton Sanders, the charge of MURDER remained an open case until April 24, 1972. No one was sure why, and no one was available to verify the information. They thought maybe the transcripts could have answered the question, but the transcripts of this particular court case had vanished. No other information was found. But the ladies were not satisfied. They still had questions. So, they decided to start probing the older family members, interviewing aunts and uncles and even cousins that may have information. What they gathered ALMOST satisfied them. A few questions still remain, but, because so few members of the family remaining were willing to discuss the events, they have to believe what they are told.

The following information was verified through interviews from people still living. It was true that there was a poker game and that a fight ensued. There are court records proving the three men served time for their actions supposedly leading to Payton's death. However, the death certificate states he died AT HOME, which means he did leave the drunken brawl alive. While sitting in the waiting room at the hospital before Gail's death, Johnny told the girls that Gail had once told his little sister Elizabeth how to cure her husband of getting drunk and beating her. Gail reportedly told Elizabeth to hide behind the door next time he came in drunk. She told her to hit him with a baseball bat, a frying pan, or whatever else she could find. This story led them to believe that Gail, herself, had tried this. She had long since told everyone that he was killed with a frying pan. Her detailed explanation of how to cure Elizabeth's husband of drinking and beating her made perfect sense to them. If she, herself had been the one to hit him in the head with a frying pan, and the girls had been taken away from her in the investigation that followed, it explained some of the questions they had about time periods that were unaccountable.

It may also explain some of the paranoia in her later years. Perhaps as she got older, her conscience began bothering her more and more. Perhaps Gail wanted to confess to someone about the truth, and that is that *"SOMETHING"* she kept trying to tell Patti Cake. Perhaps the research Patti Cake and Dottie Bug did is what Gail meant when she said *"You'll find out soon enough."* Perhaps she was right. Perhaps they have found out. However, she is no longer here to explain the truth, and no one else can confirm or deny it.

Chapter Seventeen

John Lewis "Johnny" Wyatt

PATTI CAKE AND DOTTIE BUG are now content with what they know about their mother, but they are far from satisfied because of what they don't know. They have both read the years of journals their mother kept and they both feel closer to their mother now than they ever have, but their mother was so much more complex than anyone ever gave her credit for. There was a depth to her both the girls wish they had known before she died. Perhaps if they had known more about their mother when she was living, things could have been different. But what about Johnny? What became of him? That leads to the final chapter of this story.

46 years ago, in a honky-tonk drive in restaurant on Highway 29 in College Park, he had taken over Patti Cake and Dottie Bug's lives by maneuvering into and consuming Gail's life. The day of the funeral, precious little Jenny asked her father if he wanted to move to Gainesville, Georgia and live with her. She was shocked when he said he would. Johnny asked Jenny, Dottie Bug and Patti Cake if they would come down for the next couple of days to clean their mother's belongings before he moved to live

with Jenny. Dottie Bug, Patti Cake and Jenny came to Green Valley Drive as requested. For three days they cleaned out cabinets, closets and other areas junk can gather over the years. Once they were finished, Patti Cake drove off to her own life and Dottie Bug went home to her own life, an hour away. Johnny was scheduled to leave the next morning. He had already decided that he would only take a few things. 46 years in a relationship and all he took was a bed, a television, a recliner, and a small sack of clothes and some toiletries. He told them to discard everything else.

Patti Cake woke up early that day and felt compelled to at least say good bye to him, so she drove to her mothers house, well, where her mother had lived, just to say good bye to him since it was most likely the last time she would ever see him. When Jenny and her family finished loading their truck with his few belongings, he was so ready to leave his life at Green Valley Drive that he simply hugged Patti Cake, said good bye, got in the truck and drove off to be with precious little Jenny and her family. It was the oddest day for Patti Cake. Regardless of how she felt about him, or Jenny, or what they all had been through recently, she felt hollow and numb, not sure what to think or do. As she stood there, watching Johnny drove off, Patti Cake just stood in the front yard, watching the dust that trailed behind them on that dirt road. For the first time in so long, she cried. Was it relief that the chains were finally broken, or could it be that she was sad that all those years had dissipated so quickly?

After all, five years ago, she relocated to Fayetteville, some 40 miles south of her job to be near her mother and stepfather because of their health. She uprooted her life and replanted it just seven miles from them out of loyalty to her mother. Perhaps because she was the oldest, or perhaps it was because she was the closest in proximity, during those five years, Patti Cake had devoted substantial amounts of time traveling to and from Green Valley Drive to doctors offices, pharmacies and hospitals. She allowed her mother and Johnny to absorb every moment they could by guilt tripping her into visits. She had been subjected to mental abuse from both of them as well as ridicule and alienation from her own children.

At one point in Patti Cake's life, she was so angry that she questioned her own sanity. On one particular day, she was so irritated with her mother and Johnny that by the time she got to his doctors office, she was so upset that she dropped him off at the door of the office, told him she was going shopping and she left. She was so mad when she left that she forgot how to get back into the complex. She actually forgot where she left him. She found him sitting outside an office just waiting for her. On the way home, she drove like a mad man hoping that if she scared him bad enough, he would not ask her to take him anymore. Her plan didn't work. There was a next time, and a next time. For the longest time, this seemed to have been deemed her duty.

During the past year, she and Dottie Bug were both diagnosed as clinically depressed and they were both on medications. Both of the grown women had been through so much turmoil in the past years and they both wondered just how much more they would have to endure. They prayed hard for help to get through the day and every day they asked *"What next? How much MORE, GOD?"* Soon, their prayers were answered. God said, *"It's not over, yet."*

She walked through the house and into each room. In recent years, Gail and Johnny sat all but isolated from the world for such long periods that the love they had turned sour. Bitterness over the way their lives had changed turned to an animosity that bordered on hatred. They would glare at each other across the room, seldom having much good to say to each other. Gail would claim her lack of rest was due to having to sleep with one eye open, scared he was going to kill her. Johnny would sit up late at night in his recliner, a few feet away from her hospital bed, just staring at her. God only knows what he would be thinking. Was he regretting his life? Was he plotting to kill her? Who knows? But the house had absorbed those feelings, and as she walked through the house, she couldn't help but feel the strong vibes that almost felt like evil. The house still smelled of sickness.

She stood in the dining room staring as her mind filled with the vision of that overweight shape that was her mother. The same overweight shape that she and her sister had argued with so many times in their attempts to get her up and moving around so her circulation could get better. Now there was only an empty chair on the linoleum worn bare by her mother's weight and the water bucket Johnny used to wash those red, swollen legs that were almost useless. Her mind still conjured the sight and smell of the portable potty Johnny had placed not more than three feet away from the table for her to use when she needed it. Over the years, the quality of her food had deteriorated so greatly that few people ate there, but since moving the portable potty to the dining area, no one ate there. How *could* one eat sitting next to an *outhouse?*

Patti Cake left the house, locked the door, and drove home. Johnny had simply left the house, not caring what happened to it. Patti Cakes oldest son Keith did not want to see the house simply abandoned and returned to the bank, so he discussed it with

Johnny, his mom and his 2 aunts and they all agreed that he could take over the payments and keep the house on Green Valley Drive in the family. After all, two generations of children grew up on the food grown there, and the many years of happy memories outweighed the few years of bad memories.

Life at precious little Jenny's house seemed to be good for Johnny, at least at first. It turned out that being a caretaker to someone was more than Jenny had bargained for. Her father turned out to be more burden on her than she was capable of handling. She already had her hands full with four children and the grandchildren she was helping to raise. One of her children in particular had been a challenge for Jenny all her life. Her oldest daughter was blind and severely handicapped. She lived at home with her mother and father and it was a full time job just tending to her needs. Jenny actually lived not far from Dottie Bug now, and since he still had a fondness for her, Johnny would call regularly just to keep in touch. He said the air smelled cleaner in the mountains and he was happy to be there. He was relieved to be away from the south side of town and he vowed that he would never go back again.

However, two weeks after he arrived at Jenny's house, he suffered a heart attack, followed by a series of other attacks. Each one weakened his heart more each time. Soon, Dottie Bug and Patti Cake were on another roller coaster ride. This time, it was their stepfather, who so easily drove off and out of their lives so recently. Even still, whether from pure obligation to their mother, or compassion for him woven by the years of being "their father", Patti Cake and Dottie Bug soon found themselves running to and from the hospital in Gainesville, Georgia, just like they had their mother. Isn't it ironic? Even after Gail's death, Johnny was still trying to out do her. Jenny decided that it was too much for her to handle, so she found an extended care facility a few miles from her house that would be glad to take him in. Morning Side Assisted Living Home became his new address.

He settled into a very nice room, with all the amenities he would need. Each room had its own microwave and sink, a private bathroom, and full phone and cable television access. He was tended to carefully each day with breakfast, lunches and dinners being prepared everyday. Surrounded by people his age, with illnesses ranging from mild to severe, he made friends easily. Soon, everyone there loved to talk to Johnny. Johnny started experiencing periods of highs and lows with his health. His repeated heart attacks had left his heart weak and his diabetes had caused kidney malfunctions that quickly led to the need for dialysis. His daughter, precious Jenny, lived just a few miles from him but most days he would go to dialysis alone, and periodically, with the use of his walker, he would walk himself next door to the clinic. They would assist him back to the home after the session.

Jenny was good about making sure he had food. According to Johnny, she came once a week to replenish his food supply. Once per week! Dottie Bug and Patti Cake spent a lot of time with him. They would pick him up in the mornings and he would go to Dottie Bugs house and spend the day, or they would ride to Patti Cakes house for dinner, and he even went to a 4th of July party at Patti Cakes' oldest daughters house. Johnny never lacked for attention from Patti Cake or Dottie Bug's children or grandchildren. Even for Father's Day, he received lavish gifts, clothes and cards from them. However, Jenny's children- the very children he and Gail had been so proud of and had bragged so much about for years- who also lived just a few miles from him - rarely visited their grandpa. Months would pass before he would get visits from her children. An ironic tale, huh?

Soon, Patti Cake and Dottie Bug found themselves back in the habit of devoting all their time off to Johnny, just as before. Only this time, the time they devoted to him was more grueling. Soon, their time was spent running to and from Gainesville Memorial Hospital. Each time he had a heart attack, Jenny would call her two half-sisters and say. *"This is it! He is not doing good at all! You probably need to come on up."* So Dottie Bug and Patti Cake would drop everything and they would make the trip to the hospital. This time it was Patti Cake that was over an hour away. She would meet Dottie Bug at the hospital, so sure they were going to hear death rattling in his chest, only to find him sitting up and eating as if nothing were wrong. On another occasion, he actually did die for almost three minutes before they could revive him. This time the entire family gathered thinking it was really over.

When everyone arrived at the hospital, again, everyone found him in good spirits and joking around. There were times when Dottie bug and Patti Cake would sit vigil over him while he lie there, his heart beat slowing on the monitor. They would just look at each other as they listened to the steady beep sometimes skip, or even stop. Their half sister Jenny was usually at home with her family while they took turns sleeping in a chair in his room. Yet, in a day or two, he would wake up from near death and be as alert as if he had only taken a nap. He always said he just needed that time to rejuvenate. This went on for months, and sometimes the phone would ring the very next day with the same information. It happened so frequently that Patti Cake and Dottie Bug were almost ashamed to ask for the day off. Talk about crying, *"Wolf!"* The same mind games their mother used to play. The ember of resentment from the years of mental abuse they had suffered started glowing brighter, and soon became a steady fire that burned inside their heart, again. Ironic, isn't it?

In between visits to see their stepfather, Patti Cake and Dottie Bug decided to ask him some questions about their mother. During one of the conversations, he completely blew their mind by telling them that they were not true sisters. He tried to tell them that their mother had an affair before Patti Cake was born and that she actually had a different daddy than Dottie Bug. They both felt like he may have been just trying to hurt Patti Cake. He did seem intent on breaking the bond the two sisters felt for each other. It seemed like lies to them, but the girls, never knowing for sure, could only be skeptical with an open mind. They already found out so much about their mother, his stories could be possible. Besides, it offered them something to think about and other questions for them to research.

In July 2001, for his birthday, Dottie Bug went to pick him up at Morning Side early that day. During the trip to her house, he showed Dottie Bug just how evil he could be. He began telling her stories of people in the family that surely were untrue, but what bothered her the most was how he confessed his love to her, just as he had done to her mother so many years ago. It was true! Looking back, there was no wonder why their mother wanted them out of the house. She was actually jealous of her daughters! Soon he was telling them tales of women at the nursing home fondling him, and kissing him. At first, there was humor in it and they all made light of his stories, but soon his allegations got old and it made them sick to even think that he could be that perverse.

Patti Cake's visits to Johnny became less frequent, and soon she would only ask Dottie Bug how he was doing. He started calling Patti Cakes house and leave messages like *"Patti Cake, I'm Alive,"* and he would hang up. Surely it was just more mental abuse.

Sometime in March 2002, Dottie Bug called Patti Cake with the latest stories of their stepfather. He had called to inform her of the arrangements he made with a crematorium in Gainesville. There would be no funeral service and no flowers. Instead, his "real" daughter would simply call them when he had died. Dottie tried to explain that a funeral is not for the dead, but a chance for the living to place closure on the event. He didn't want anyone to be around. He was acting just as he had when he was younger. If there was going to be no funeral, Patti Cake and her two daughters felt the need to see him before he died. They went to Dottie Bugs house so they could all ride together.

They met him in the parlor at Morning Side where he had been waiting for them. He got up to greet them, but he didn't seem to have good balance. Ever since he lost sight in his left eye, his gaze could be eerie, but today the stare from that bloodshot eye was especially hollow. It seemed strange being there that day. When they got back to his room they chatted a bit and were soon talking about his decision to be cremated. They had not been in his room long before he said he had to get some air. They left his room, stepping down the hall a bit to the outside patio. They all took their seats around Johnny and Patti Cake decided she wanted to talk about their investigation. They needed him to clarify a few things. She began reporting the facts they had uncovered. For a few minutes, he offered some explanations about some of the events, confirming some of the stories that others in the family had given to the women during their investigations, but somehow they had touched on something he didn't want to discuss.

Something upset him. He became agitated and soon became irate with them. He told them to let the past be the past! No sooner had the words left his lips that Dottie Bug jumped up and started screaming at him. *"It's a damned shame that we have lived 50 years with a pack of lies! We are two grown women who don't know where we came from or even who our mother really was! Why would she bury our sister with no identity as if the little baby never existed? Why did she murder our father and what exactly happened to us when we were kids to cause us to be taken away from her? How could you want us to forget it? We deserve that much and we WILL find out!"*

At that moment, Patti Cake was so proud of her sister. For a second, Johnny sat there, looking almost ashamed. He knew the game was over. He knew these two grown women had found out what so many people had hidden for so many years. But he would never admit it. Instead, he stood up and said, *"I am tired now. Its time for you to leave."* At his request, on that sunny day in March 2002, Dottie Bug, Patti Cake and her daughters left Johnny standing there, all alone at Morning Side Assisted Living Home.

On the way home, they were all talking at one time about what had just happened. Dottie Bug felt a huge weight lifted from her shoulders. That very day, Patti Cake and Dottie Bug made themselves a pact. No longer would they be bound by their past. They had already been through so much with their mother and now they had been cleansed of their duties to their stepfather. The next day, Johnny called Patti Cake's son Keith and told him what had happened. Johnny expressed to Keith that he didn't want to be bothered by anyone anymore. Keith called his mother shortly after and told her and his aunt Dottie Bug they should let it go.

That happened to he the last mind game he ever played on Patti Cake and Dottie Bug. Both of them could now go on with their lives and heal the wounds that had hurt them for so many years.

They were no longer *"Lost in the Sins of Their Mother!"*

Prologue

John Lewis Wyatt, Jr.

Passed away on Sunday, September 8, 2002
At 7:27am at his home
At Morningside Assisted Living Home
In Gainesville, GA.

His battle against his many health issues for the past years finally took its toll. He simply got tired.

He wanted no service to be held, and no fuss be made over his passing. His daughter, Jennifer Lynn Wyatt-Simpson, her husband Lonnie and her children and grandchildren will have a small family gathering on Tuesday, September 10, 2002 at her home.

His last wish was to be cremated and be taken to gulf coast of Florida to be spread into the waves. Jennifer will take Johnny to St. George Island in October.

Now, the story is complete.

Goodbye, "Daddy"

Printed in the United States
17854LVS00005B/280-327